Whinnies on the Wind
Volume 5

Winter of Sinking Waters

by

Angela Dorsey

D1262060

www.ponybooks.com

Copyright © Angela Dorsey 2012
www.angeladorsey.com

Original Title: Winter of Sinking Waters
Cover Design: 2012 Marina Miller
Printed in the USA, 2012

ISBN: 978-1-927100-25-7

Enchanted Pony Books
www.ponybooks.com

Winter of Sinking Waters

Angela Dorsey

Also at *Enchanted Pony Books*

Whinnies on the Wind Series

Winter of the Crystal Dances
Spring of the Poacher's Moon
Summer of Wild Hearts
Autumn in Snake Canyon
Winter of Sinking Waters
Spring of Secrets
Summer of Desperate Races
Autumn of Angels
Winter of the Whinnies Brigade

Sun Series

Sun Catcher
Sun Chaser
Sun Seeker

Horse Guardian Series

Dark Fire	Rattlesnake Rock
Desert Song	Sobekkare's Revenge
Condor Mountain	Mystic Tide
Swift Current	Silver Dream
Gold Fever	Fighting Chance
Slave Child	Wolf Chasm

Single Titles
Abandoned

Still night
Ice glistens
Moon lights
Wilds listen

Cows shuffle
Hear noise
Steps muffled
Listen, poise

Paws tread
Creak snow
Firm stead
Stalk slow

Danger near?
Should we fear?

Chapter 1

First, Mom offered to make us cookies before she left us at Kestrel's house.

"No, thanks, Mom. We're not hungry," I said, even though the second she left, we'd make something thoroughly sweet and gooey to eat.

"My mom already made us some cookies," added Kestrel, my best friend. "But thanks anyway."

Then, Mom checked the radiophone battery just in case we needed to phone Kestrel's parents, who had left early that morning and were already hours away.

Yes, Mom, it's still charged, just like it was when you checked it five minutes ago. I didn't say this out loud, of course. I'm not completely stupid.

As she put on her coat by the door, she told me for about the hundredth time, "Ride straight home if you need anything, Evy. *Anything.* I mean it. Anything at all."

"Of course I will," I said, as soothingly as possible. "But nothing's going to happen. We're going to be fine. It's not like we're going to be alone for a week or anything." Though we were going to be alone for an afternoon, a night, a day, another night, *and* the next morning. The thought gave me both a thrill of excitement and a shiver of uneasiness. Kestrel's ranch was far away from everything – but still, it wasn't as remote as I was used to. Our cabin was even farther into the bush. It had to be Mom's worrying that was making me nervous.

1

Finally, with nothing reasonable left to say or check or offer, Mom opened the door and walked out onto the porch. The extremely cold porch. It's winter here in the British Columbian interior now, after all. My best friend Kestrel and I followed her without bothering to put on our coats; I mean, how long does it take to get on a horse and head out? Not long, right?

Ha! I should have known better. Kestrel and I stopped at the top step while Mom descended and approached Cocoa, her ride home. Then with her hand on Cocoa's neck, she turned. More directives and worries and orders and concerns spewed from her mouth as I nodded and made agreeable noises and did my best to stop my teeth from clanking together from the cold. And finally, *finally*, she reluctantly climbed into Cocoa's saddle.

There was a long pause as she stared at us. "Are you one hundred percent sure that you're going to be okay here alone, girls?" she asked, her gaze drilling holes into my eyes.

"Yes. We'll be fine."

"Yes," Kestrel repeated beside me, her voice quavering with the cold.

"Because if you're even a little teensy tiny bit afraid, I'm happy to stay."

No offense to Mom or anything, but that was the *last* thing we wanted. "We're not scared, Mom. I promise," I whined. *Go already*. "Everything's going to be fine." Then Kestrel and I waited, shivering and clutching our arms and chattering our teeth, as Mom sat on Cocoa, trying to think of something more to say, something more to offer, anything that might give her an excuse to put off leaving.

Nervous and lonely, said Rusty, my gelding, speaking directly into my brain.

I looked toward the barn to see his adorable gray face peering at us from between the poles of his corral – and suddenly, I clued in. Okay, so I'm thick. Mom might be worried about leaving us alone at the ranch, but I'd totally overlooked that she was probably going to miss me too. I'd be here with Kestrel and the three horses, and she'd be all by herself. Well, she'd have Loonie, our old dog, plus Cocoa, but it's not like she and Cocoa and Loonie have many in-depth conversations. She might have Tumpoo too – that's my yearling moose calf – but he'd been spending lots of time in the bush lately, turning back to the wild. Mom would be lucky if he *didn't* come home for a visit while I was gone. He's even brattier than Twilight, my wonderfully intrepid mustang filly.

I glanced back at Rusty for a millisecond. He was eating again, confident I'd understood him.

"You'll feel better when you get home and start your next painting, Mom," I said, hoping to console her. "Just think of all the uninterrupted time you'll have. No one to bother you. No one to cook for."

Her face froze for a second, then she looked away as if embarrassed. I guess obvious sympathy from her daughter wasn't what she was going for.

When she spoke again, her voice was strong. "You girls be good, now." Then she turned Cocoa toward the big ranch gates.

"Bye," Kestrel called to her.

Mom stopped Cocoa and looked back. "Now remember, if you need anything…"

"We'll ride straight to you," I finished for her. "We promise."

3

Mom nodded and blinked a few times in the second it took her to stare at me as if she was memorizing every tiny detail of my face. I kept my gaze steady – I could show no weakness or she'd be off Cocoa as quick as I could say *Twilight is a brat*.

I felt Twilight's smirk in my mind. She'd been eavesdropping on my thoughts again. Couldn't a person have any privacy?

Finally, Mom asked Cocoa to walk on and we watched her ride away from us through the snow, looking small and blue – because of her coat, not the cold – on her big chocolate-coloured mare. James, Kestrel's collie, followed them to the ranch gates, sniffing Cocoa's tracks as if they were the most fascinating things in the world.

Mom turned in the saddle just before getting out of sight and waved to us with her gloved hand. We waved back and Kestrel called James, who of course ignored her until she called him a second time. Then Mom was out of sight and we were alone.

The sudden stillness after all that talking seemed strange. I could hear the breeze rubbing pine branches together in the big tree beside Kestrel's house. I could hear myself breathing.

"Awesome," Kestrel said. "No parents. No sisters. No one who can boss us around."

I laughed. "Well, Rusty and Twilight are kind of bossy." And just in case you didn't catch it after Rusty's hint, I can talk to horses telepathically, or I can talk to Rusty and Twilight and a mustang mare called Wildfire telepathically. With most others, I can communicate through emotions and sensations. And don't ask why I've been blessed – or cursed – with this gift, because I don't know. I was just born that way.

4

"Yeah, but we don't have to listen to them," said Kestrel and grinned at me.

James trotted the last couple feet to the porch, his paws softly crunching the snow. Then he leaped up the steps and curled into his bed by the door, tucking his paws into the long hair under his tummy. A big doggy sigh was next. Obviously, he'd had enough excitement for one day.

Not enough for us, though.

First, we were going to make a cake and maybe some fudge too. Then we were going to fire up the generator and watch a DVD and eat our goodies for lunch. Yum!

After the movie, we'd spend some time with our horses and do our chores – which were the reasons we were staying at Kestrel's house while her parents were gone. Someone had to take care of the cattle, all one hundred and twenty of them! But enough about responsibilities. After chores, we planned to eat supper and then maybe do a bit of snooping – I love looking through Kestrel's older sisters' stuff – and finally, before our *very* late bedtime, we planned to play some really loud music and do lots of running around, dancing, and screaming. Sounds divine, doesn't it? Oh yeah!

"Are you receiving more psychic horse messages?" Kestrel asked beside me.

"No, just zoning about how much fun we're going to have." My stomach was a hollow pit in my middle, crying out for cake. Time to get busy measuring, mixing, and looking for interesting additions to our culinary masterpiece. Maybe Elaine, Kestrel's mom, had some jellybeans hidden in a cupboard.

After we stirred and snooped for yummy things to add to our cake (we found sour gummies – score!), we poured the batter into a pan and put it in the oven. Baking it was the hard part. Because we both live in the bush and it's too hard to fire up the generator every time you want to cook something, Kestrel's stove was a wood cook stove. That meant a fire heated the oven, which made it a little harder to bake a cake. But not impossible. You just add wood when the thermostat gets too low.

Unfortunately, we weren't sure what to do when the temperature got too high, and finally had to open the oven door to release some of the heat. Long story short, we let out too much hot air. As the side of the cake closest to the fire started to turn black, the other side remained a sticky goo. We finally decided to take the poor thing out of the oven, hoping the strip down the middle between burnt and raw would be salvageable.

It was. In fact, it was even more than okay. It was great. Then we spooned the raw part into bowls, added some more candy, decided it was as good as fudge, and prepared to zone in front of the TV.

First, Kestrel had to dart outside to fire up the generator so we had electricity. While she headed around the side of the house to the generator shed, I slipped on my coat, hat, scarf, and mittens, skipped down the porch steps, then jogged toward Rusty and Twilight's corral.

The sun felt good on my face even as the sharp air bit at my cheeks and nose. Twilight watched me approach from the gate while Rusty napped broadside to the barn wall, soaking in the weak winter sun. He not only looked peaceful, but felt it too. His drowsiness of mind was like being cuddled in a warm comforter.

I reached the gate, quietly opened it, and slipped through. "Are you being a good girl, Twilight?" I whispered, so I wouldn't disturb Rusty's peace.

Twilight snorted softly and nuzzled my shoulder, or rather the layers of clothing that covered my shoulder.

"I hope you don't mind being locked up, beauty." Of course, she couldn't understand me – I wasn't speaking telepathically and she didn't know English – but I didn't really want to know how much she disliked being confined. I already knew she despised it. At home, Twilight is allowed to come and go as she pleases and she definitely likes it that way.

The rumble of the generator cut through the stillness. Rusty opened his eyes, so of course I had to hurry over to give him a snuggle too. His long winter hair made him look so warm and fuzzy, so I pulled off my mittens and sank my fingers into the fluffy softness I never tired of.

"Ready, Evy?" Kestrel's shout came from the house.

I gave her a wave so she'd know I heard, then walked back to Twilight, still standing at the gate, to give her a quick hug. She smelled so nice, so clean and fresh and wintery and horsey, all at once. Then, because I knew Kestrel would ask how her horse was doing, I zoned in to Twitchy's mind.

Inside the barn, Kestrel's old bay mare was having a snooze too. I moved in closer to her fuzzy thoughts and little white flashes of movement darted through my mind. I moved in closer.

A rabbit! She was dreaming about a white rabbit, and in the dream she chased after it – cool! Twitchy was in Wonderland. I had to tell Kestrel.

Reluctantly, I pulled away from Twilight, gave her a parting pat, and hurried back through the gate, making sure it was closed and latched behind me. James came to meet me, and then turned to walk beside me as I dangled my still bare fingers over his head and rubbed his ears.

"I can't wait to watch this movie. I've been saving it forever," Kestrel said when I reached her.

I grinned. "Twitchy has her own movie going on. Just wait until I tell you."

Kestrel was still giggling when we reached the house. Inside, we brushed snow from our coats, slid them off, and dumped them on the floor near the door.

"Weird," my friend said as she stared down at her coat. "I can almost hear Mom telling me to hang it up."

"Not so strange. I hear Rusty telling me what to do all the time."

Kestrel laughed and we moved toward the living room. "Yeah, but he really *does* talk in your head. If my mom could talk to me in my head, I'd..." She paused, unable to think of anything horrible enough. "Well, at least Rusty isn't telling you to pick up your dirty socks or anything."

"True."

She glanced back at her coat again.

"Either hang it up or forget about it," I said and shrugged my shoulders so she'd know I didn't care which one she chose. I, however, had no problem leaving my coat on the floor.

She sat down on the couch, picked up the remote – and then jumped up to rush toward the coat heap. I sighed and trailed after her. I guess I had to be neat too.

Once the coats were put away to Kestrel's satisfaction, we were finally ready. The movie was instantly exciting and awesome. The couch and blankets were cozy and comfy. My best friend's comments were fun and witty. Twilight and Rusty were safely contained outside. We had no parents around to tell us to clean up our mess in the kitchen. Could life get any better?

Just to make sure things were going to remain good, I reached out to Twilight again mid-movie. Frustration touched me and even a little bit of anger – and then she realized I was in her head and she shoved me out. I smiled. If Twilight was frustrated, that was a good thing. It meant she wasn't succeeding at whatever mischief she was trying to create. I relaxed a bit more deeply into the couch. Ahhh.

The movie was watched and the cake, batter, and gummies completely consumed. When the credits started to roll, Kestrel stood, stretched, and yawned. I did the same without standing.

"Back in a minute," said Kestrel, and moved lethargically toward the door to go outside and turn off the generator.

"Sure," I said and leaned back, totally relaxed. I reached toward Twilight – only to meet a mental wall. My shoulders stiffened. What was she up to? She'd been shutting me out for a while now. Something had to be afoot.

Twilight? I asked Rusty.

I felt him stir a hoof. The sun wasn't as warm on his side now. It must be moving toward the horizon. Which meant we'd need to get out there soon and give those one hundred and twenty cows their supper. Which would take an hour or so. Groan.

Gone.

"What?" The word popped from my mouth, but of course no one was there to answer. *What?* I asked Rusty.

Gone. He felt as surprised as I did. I guess he'd been sleeping when she'd somehow escaped their corral.

I jumped off the couch and hurried through the kitchen, grabbing my coat on my way out the door. Onto the porch, down the stairs, and… stop. I shoved my arms into my coat sleeves as I stared across the ranch yard. Everything looked fine. Rusty was staring at me over the bars of a closed gate. It was true that Twilight wasn't beside him, but couldn't she be inside the lean-to, out of sight?

But then, why doubt Rusty? That was just silly.

The generator's roar hiccupped and died, and moments later Kestrel walked around the side of the house. "What's up?" she asked.

"Something's wrong. Rusty says that Twilight's gone." I started walking across the snowy yard and Kestrel fell in beside me.

"But the gate's still closed. Is she, like, magic now? Twilight, the great disappearing horse?"

"Maybe she broke down the fence on the other side," I said, heartily wishing that wasn't what happened. We'd have to fix it before Kestrel's parents came home and that might be hard. The fence was high and strong. In fact, I didn't see how Twilight, a spindly two-year-old, could possibly break it down – but then this was my mischievous filly we were talking about. She had ways of doing naughty things.

"Look," Kestrel said, pointing. Tracks. Twilight's tracks. They had to be, because the snow had been new and fresh there when we'd ridden in. And the tracks led from the closed gate straight to the *almost* closed door of the feed shed.

I made a noise of frustration and fear, and ran toward the door. How long had she been in there? Even Rusty

10

wouldn't know because he'd been sleeping. She could be all colicky and twisted up inside. Or she could be foundering. My heart hammered like a scared rabbit's as I pushed the door open.

Yup, there she was, head deep in a bag of grain.

"Twilight!" I shrieked.

Twilight shot into the air, her mane a spray of darkness around her shocked eyes. She landed lightly and spun to face me in the small space, agile as could be. Then she snorted. *Oh, you*, she thought. Then she plunged her head back into the feed sack.

"No!" I yelled and sprang toward her.

Twilight jerked back and jumped out of my reach.

Too much makes sick! Might kill!

She snorted again and I could feel the struggle in her mind as she weighed my words against the deliciousness that filled her mouth.

Too much might make lame. Forever lame.

I felt something touch my hand and looked back to see Kestrel pushing a halter at me. "We should put this on her in here, where she can't get away," she said quietly.

I nodded and took the halter. Twilight backed another step. Her eyes narrowed. I didn't need to read her thoughts to know she had no intention of letting me put that halter on her head.

I sighed. Why did she have to be so difficult? Independence was a great thing, but only to a certain degree. If only she'd listen to reason. I reached out to her mind. *Come with me.*

Irritation prickled back at me.

Please? I thought, trying another tack.

She snorted and pinned her ears back.

"I don't think she's going to let me put a halter on her," I said to Kestrel.

"So how do we get her out?"

"That's not the problem. The problem is how to make sure she's okay if she won't let us near her."

"Let's just get her outside first. Then maybe we can talk her into letting us examine her."

"Okay," I said, though we really didn't have much of a choice. If I went toward Twilight with the halter right now, she might even nip me. She was pretty adamant about her refusals and had never backed down as long as I'd known her.

Kind of peeved about her obstinacy and not wanting her to notice my defeat, I thought to her in no uncertain terms that she could either wear the halter out of the feed shed or walk outside by herself.

Of course, she chose to leave by herself. As she walked past me, her ears back and head high – just in case I made a wild leap and got the halter over her nose, I guess – she cast a single thought at me. *Mean.*

You did dangerous thing.

Another snort, and then she sashayed past me, flipping her tail in my face. Nice.

"What a brat," said Kestrel as we followed her outside.

The moment Twilight left the feed shed she pranced away from us, arrogant as can be. *Not sick,* she said to me, just in case I didn't get why she was making a point of acting so bouncy.

I bit down my thoughts and watched her dance through the snow, both relieved that she seemed okay for now and furious at her for being so cocky about it. She edged toward the porch where James slept, snow flying from around her high-stepping legs. When she reached the house, she nickered to the sleepy collie and shook her ebony mane in glee. James looked up and yawned, then stood up and retreated deeper onto the porch. Apparently he wasn't into playing with her, probably sensing all the extra energy from the oats.

Kestrel laughed and Twilight took the sudden sound as an opportunity to spazz out. She erupted like a bucking bronco, scattering snow as she leapt across the yard.

I scowled. "I need to feel her coronet band and ear tips to see if she's feverish. And I have to find some way to control her so I can actually do something if she gets sick."

"The snow is probably good for her if she's foundering. If her hooves stay cool, the coffin bone might not rotate or sink even if she does get laminitis," Kestrel responded. "We need to feed the cows before it gets dark anyway. Maybe when we're done she'll be calmer and we can check her out."

"As long as she's not still completely unreasonable, I'll be happy." I watched my filly gallop away through the open ranch gates. Just before her golden behind disappeared into the forest on the other side of the snowbound road, she flicked up her heels. Irksome horse! I turned away. "So let's get it done. The cows, I mean."

Kestrel made a wry face. "You wouldn't sound so eager if you knew how much work it was."

"How much work can it be, throwing out a few bales of hay?"

Um, turns out, a *lot* of work. First we loaded about 40 bales in the back of their beat up flatbed truck. That took almost an hour. Then Kestrel drove it out to the big enclosure where the cows waited impatiently. Yes,

Kestrel drives. She and her sisters all learned at about age eight. Unfortunately, before Elaine left she made Kestrel promise that she wouldn't let *me* drive the truck. I guess she's had to tell me "no" too many times to trust me not to ask Kestrel. And since I wasn't allowed to try driving, I was stuck opening and shutting gates and throwing the hay to the cows. Whoopee.

I got out of the truck and approached the cow's gate. A hundred and twenty pairs of eyes watched me intently from the other side of the metal rails. Some of them leaned, pushing the gate taut against the latch that held it shut. It didn't take a genius to realize that the second I opened the gate, there would be a stampede toward the hay – and I would be between the herd and its object of desire.

"Just hit the latch and run!" Kestrel yelled from her open window.

No prob. Just hit the latch and run as if a stampeding herd of cattle wasn't mere inches behind me with their sharp, cloven hooves and hungry eyes.

Taking a deep breath, I swatted the bit of metal that was holding the gate in place, turned, and ran!

Halfway to the truck, I noticed Kestrel's laughing face through the windshield. I didn't slow but I turned my head. One hundred and twenty pairs of disappointed eyes looked at me from behind metal bars. The latch hadn't released. I tossed Kestrel a friends-shouldn't-laugh-at-friends look and turned back.

I gathered my courage again as I retraced my steps, then kicked at the snow around the gate until I found what I needed, a nice sized rock. With the rock firmly in hand, I took careful aim and whacked the latch with the rock.

The gate shot toward me like a big metal fist. I jumped back just in time to avoid being knocked down, only to face something far more scary. Heavy brown and white bodies jostled and shoved their way through the sudden opening, hay lust shining in their eyes. I stumbled backward as they rumbled toward me like a living tidal wave on hooves, shouldering and shoving and bawling, then I turned tail and ran for the truck, praying like crazy that I wouldn't slip, wouldn't trip, and that for once, my clumsiness wouldn't decide to intervene.

Chapter 2

The herd thundered mere inches behind me. I swear I could feel their breath on the back of my neck. I raced past the truck cab, past the rear tire, then swung up onto the back bales of hay. The voracious beasts started ripping into the lower bales as I scrambled up the pile. Then, just as I reached the top, Kestrel drove forward. I teetered on the hay pinnacle, looking down in horror as the sea of brown below me grunted and shoved and slobbered, and then finally I caught my balance.

The truck swayed forward over the rough ground and the herd followed us back through the gate. Once inside their enclosure, I cut the strings on the first bale, pulled them off, and threw the loose chunks into the waiting horde. My muscles thrummed with the thrill of being almost trampled, and though it was winter and *cold* outside I felt warm. I watched the hay disappear beneath the apparently famished creatures, completely engulfed as if it had never existed.

Kestrel revved the engine and the truck crept a few feet forward through the snow. Another bale thrown down. Wait for Kestrel to drive forward and throw down another. Now multiply that by twenty, and we were still only halfway done. My muscles were no longer thrumming; they were screaming. Only a few of the cattle were following us now, so I slowed down. Thirty bales over the edge, and the cattle were all behind us in a long narrow row of milling red and white. Seeing the end in sight, I decided to really work on the last ten bales and get the job finished.

Six bales to go – and that's when I heard her.

Bear!

I honed into Twilight's vision to see absolutely nothing. She only smelled the bear, and – weird – this was a bear smell she recognized. It was the same grizzly that had chased Tumpoo just a couple of months ago. I remembered it clearly. It hadn't seemed the brightest bear in the world because it didn't notice Edward, also known as the piñata, hanging out of a sapling. This was a good thing, because otherwise Edward might've become its dinner, and even if Edward is a thief who stole thousands of dollars from my mom, being eaten by a grizzly would've been a bit of overkill as far as punishment goes. No pun intended.

Kestrel stopped the truck and jumped down from the cab. "Why don't you get inside the truck and warm up," she offered. "I can do the last bales."

"Hey, Twilight just smelled that bear that chased Tumpoo last fall."

Kestrel climbed up on the flatbed. "Weird. He's not hibernating?"

"Maybe he was dreaming of the Edward piñata and decided to find a mid-winter snack," I said, handing her the twine cutter and then shoving my hands into my pockets. I'd wait for the job to be finished before I went inside the truck cab. "Or maybe it's because he smells really gross. Twilight thinks he reeks like the back end of a dead skunk. Maybe he needed to get out of his den for some fresh air."

"I hope he doesn't start causing trouble," said Kestrel, ignoring my joke. A line appeared on her forehead as she sliced the twine holding the last few bales together. "We don't have anything that can scare off a grizzly, not until Mom and Dad get home. I'm not allowed to use the rifles." She pushed a bale over the side of the truck. "And they're locked up anyway."

"He probably just woke up for a short stroll. I bet he'll be sound asleep again by dark."

Together, we kicked the rest of the hay off the sides and back of the flatbed.

"Cow cows!" yelled Kestrel, using the call that the cows knew meant *food*. One super pregnant cow left the crowd and swayed toward us – I swear, she looked as though she was going to have triplets at any second – and then another followed her to the last bales. At least these two wouldn't have to fight for their hay.

As I watched the super big cow lumber our way, I couldn't help but worry. If the grizzly was out of his den because he was hungry and decided to go after some of the more heavily pregnant cows, there would be nothing we could do to stop him. We had no rifle to scare him off. There were no adults around. The only person we could phone that was close enough to help was Charlie, the Wild Horse Ranger, but Kestrel's ranch was so remote it would take him more than two hours to get here. *If* he wasn't off somewhere. Charlie's job is to watch over the mustangs, so he spends most of his time in the bush.

To ride to get Mom and come all the way back would take at least two hours too. Things would be a lot easier if we could just phone her, but that's the thing about my Mom. She refuses to get a phone. She's a hermit and doesn't like to talk with anyone other than Kestrel's family, though lately she's been forced to accept that Charlie might drop by to say hello to me now and then and catch up on my mustang news. So Kestrel's family and Charlie equal the limit of our social circle.

Well, I guess she used to see Edward, her agent, twice a year too, when he'd come to pick up her paintings, but ever since he stole that money from us, we haven't heard a whisper from him.

Anyway, Mom being a hermit was really a drag sometimes, not only socially, but when things went wrong too. But this time, things were even *more* inconvenient than the amount of time it would take to go get her. I mean, what could I tell her when I saw her? Certainly not the truth, that Twilight had smelled a bear. Mom doesn't know about my horse telepathy and she'd go hysterical on me if I told her. Believe me, I know. I tried to tell her once, when I was little, and she totally freaked until I was able to convince her I was just joking.

"Don't worry. Everything will be okay," I said.

Kestrel looked at me and raised an eyebrow. "What do you mean?"

Oh great. So I was the only one obsessing about the bear? Except now my worries were going to infect Kestrel and make her uneasy too. Unless... "Everything will be okay with Twilight," I said, then sighed for real. I actually was still very worried about my filly.

Kestrel looked at me sympathetically. I guess people are allowed to act weird when motivated by concern for their horses. "Of course she'll be okay. We just have to keep an eye on her so if anything bad starts to happen, we're right there to help her."

I nodded, eager to believe Kestrel's words.

"Let's get inside. I'm freezing."

We jumped down from the flatbed, sending the closest super-pregnant cow prancing away with her tail in the air and her belly wobbling like a huge water-

19

filled balloon. I hurried to the door of the truck and lurched inside. Ah, warmth.

"You think she'll let us check her now?" Kestrel asked, climbing in the driver's side. She shut her door and ground the stick shift into first gear.

"I'll ask her." I sent my horse radar out to Twilight. She was busy following the bear's trail now – and his tracks were moving away from the ranch. So my worries *were* for nothing. What a relief!

But what a weird horse. Every other horse I knew would be going the opposite direction as fast as their legs would carry them. Not Twilight.

Feel sick? I asked my beautiful mustang filly.

No.

Can we check?

Her response was sudden annoyance. Apparently, she was having fun and didn't want to turn back.

Please? I asked before I remembered that Twilight didn't really get human politeness. Thankfully, she didn't bother responding, which was much better than giving me some snarky thought in return. *Treat?* I added, just in case that could entice her after her oat binge.

Twilight stopped. *Oats?*

"Can I give her a cookie if she comes back?" I asked Kestrel. I know it's not healthy but I didn't want to give her more oats. That was the last thing she needed, and besides, it was the principle of the thing. She didn't deserve oats after breaking into the feed shed.

"Sure," said Kestrel, shrugging that she couldn't care less. "Mom made lots."

"Thanks." *Cookie*, I thought to Twilight.

My filly spun around and trotted back toward the ranch house, abandoning the bear's trail without a second thought. I was a little surprised. I didn't realize she liked cookies so much. Probably because she usually declined the ones that I made.

She loped into the ranch yard looking perfectly hale and hearty just as Kestrel was parking the truck. Not a tender step to be seen. I was immediately cheered. Maybe she was going to be fine. Lucky girl!

Reluctantly, I opened the door. Winter cold slapped me as I slid out of the truck and we crunched through the snow toward Twilight. She stopped and sighed, resigned to the ignoble fate of being examined, all in the name of cookies. As we approached her, I nabbed the halter from where it hung near the feed room door, then slipped the soft nylon onto her head and handed the lead rope to Kestrel. She stroked Twilight's gold and black face as I bent to feel along the filly's coronet band.

Was it warmer than usual? I didn't think so. Her ear tips, too, seemed normal. But a fever could come on fast. Next I pressed my ear against her side. Grumbles and rumbles flowed through the walls of her stomach and into my ear. So far, so good.

How much did eat?

Not enough.

I rolled my eyes and patted her side as I turned to Kestrel. "Do you know how much was in that bag before she ate anything?"

"It was three quarters full, I think."

And it had been about half empty when we interrupted Twilight's binge. Half empty. A 50 pound bag. For the first time ever, I wished I was better at math. Three quarters was thirty seven and a half pounds, half was twenty five pounds, so that meant

Twilight had eaten twelve and a half pounds of grain? I redid the numbers in my head. Yes, that was right.

So how many gallons was that?

Uh... lots.

"It really is amazing how she knew to shut the gate to her corral and then the door to the feed shed so we wouldn't notice her in there right away," Kestrel said as I checked Twilight's back legs. No heat there either. Maybe my intrepid filly had lucked out.

"She's way too smart for her own good," I said aloud to my friend, then thought the same thing to Twilight and added *sneaky too.*

My horse ignored me.

"Good thing the movie was over when it was too. Another hour and she would have finished the bag."

"I know." I shuddered and it wasn't from the cold seeping through my winter clothing. "I'm going to get up during the night to check on her too, just in case." I took the lead rope to guide Twilight back to the corral.

"I'll go get her cookie," said Kestrel.

"I'll come with you. Just let me put Twilight in with Rusty first."

Cookie? Twilight snorted a warning. She wanted it *now* and of course she didn't understand our human language.

One minute. As if she knew how long a minute was. *In house.*

Hurry, she said and flapped her lips together.

When I led her through the gate, she didn't seem to be too upset about being back where she started, probably because she was planning on escaping as soon as Kestrel and I were back in the house for the night. But there would be no way for her to get out of the corral when I was finished with it. Not this time. The gate was going to be tied shut, with the knot on the outside. Carefully, I guarded my thoughts so Twilight wouldn't suspect. However, the second I closed the gate behind her she noticed my smugness. Her suspicion grew as I unbuckled her halter and let it slide from her head, then opened the gate just enough to squeeze myself through.

Cookie.

Yes. Soon.

Kestrel came back to the kitchen with me, then stayed inside to warm up while I headed back outside with three cookies, two in my hands for Twilight and Rusty, and one in my pocket for Twitchy, Kestrel's old bay mare. I didn't want her to feel left out.

James caught the scent of cookie as I walked past his bed and bounded to his paws. He pranced beside me, his tail like a sail in the air, and inhaled the sweet cookie scent. Maybe Kestrel would let me give him one when we got back to the house.

Both Twilight and Rusty pushed their cute faces between the fence rails and their breath mist rose into the air as they watched me carry their treats toward them. Their lips twitched eagerly. When I held out their cookies on flat palms, Twilight snapped up her cookie as if she was afraid it would vanish at any moment, while Rusty lipped his up like a gentleman. I stroked their two faces as they chewed rapturously, then climbed through the fence and walked into the lean-to that was their shelter at the back of the barn. Their water was still good, not frozen yet because of the protection of the overhang. By morning though, it would be hard as a rock and I'd have to knock out the ice and haul them some more. They still had hay, both in their mangers and out in the corral.

A whinny came from inside the barn. Kestrel liked to keep Twitchy loose in the big arena because then she had lots of room to run, plus was still under shelter. Not that Twitchy liked to run much. Ha ha. But still, it was healthier for her than staying outside on the super cold days. She got twinges of arthritis in her front shoulders now, a new thing that had started just this winter, and the cold was hard on her. Living indoors really helped her, and Kestrel didn't mind scooping the poop.

I opened the big door enough to slide inside. A dark horse moved in the shadows in front of me.

"Twitchy? You hungry, girl?" A silly question. Of course she was hungry. Twitchy was *always* hungry. I reached out and my fingers sank into the big pouf of hair that was her forelock. She nickered gently as I rubbed her forehead, then I gave her the cookie and the soft sound of chewing floated around me. I gave her a pat before sliding between the doors again. Kestrel had already given her her hay and checked her water.

I turned the corner of the barn to see Twilight fiddling with the catch on the gate. It sure hadn't taken her long to make her escape attempt. "Hey!" Twilight flung up her head as I ran toward the gate, then she trotted away from me, snorting.

I grabbed the lead rope hanging on the fence and tied the gate shut with a triple knot. "You're such a pest, Twilight. Why can't you be more like Rusty and Twitchy?" Of course I didn't say it to her with my thoughts, because I didn't *really* mean it – I liked her just the way she was, or most of the time anyway – even though she was now glaring at me from inside the corral. Moments later, I was hurrying back across the yard, hoping she'd be over her pique by morning.

24

At the porch steps, I braved the plummeting temperature to pause and look back over the ranch yard. Sunset light slanted across the snow and Rusty and Twilight glowed from inside their corral. In the distant enclosure, the cows shone like rubies as they chewed their supper of wild hay. The evergreens behind them glowed like dark emeralds, and the clouds reflected pink coral, purple amethyst, and yellow sapphire.

My heart burned in my chest as I inhaled the beauty saturating the sharp air. I could almost feel it soaking into my skin and being absorbed through my eyes. A fierce pride swelled inside me. This was my home. This was my land. Well, not literally. This ranch belonged to Kestrel's family – but my home would look as stunning right now. It was the north country that was amazing, such a harsh, magnificent land.

A cold wet nose touched my hand and I looked down to see James, hopefulness lingering in his eyes. Oh yeah, his cookie. I bent to give him a snuggle. "I'll ask Kestrel if it's okay," I murmured as I sank my fingers into his soft, thick coat.

Before going inside, I took one more look at the amazing sunset. It was already fading and soon the sky would be dark. I'd have to use a flashlight when I came out to check on Twilight in the night. My midnight visit would probably be short because, thank goodness, my filly seemed okay. She even looked somewhat resigned to her fate as she placidly ate her hay beside Rusty.

But I knew Twilight. She could also be trying to trick me into a false sense of security so she could later enact some dastardly plan.

I know, I'm too suspicious. After all, she's *just* a horse. Yeah, right. Just a very smart, confident, and adventurous horse who doesn't acknowledge me as her boss. Correction: doesn't acknowledge *anyone* as her boss.

After James got his cookie, Kestrel and I thought about making supper but we were still too full from all the cake, so we did a bit of snooping instead. That turned out to be a disaster. If Kestrel felt guilty leaving her coat on the floor, you can imagine how she felt snooping in her big sister's room. But honestly, it wasn't just Kestrel. I felt kind of bad too. I kept thinking of how I'd feel if I had a little sister and she snooped through my stuff, and besides, it wasn't as much fun when we weren't in imminent danger of being caught. Within a few minutes, we sheepishly closed her sister's bedroom door and went to find something more fun to do, which turned out to be singing to Kestrel's battery powered CD's and making weird shadows on the walls as we danced in the lantern light. Then, cookies for our very late supper, and afterward, more general goofing off.

When we finally stopped, I was ready to crawl into my sleeping bag. However, the day wasn't over yet because then we talked for hours in the dark about our wonderful horses, our past adventures, the rodeo coming up next summer, and stuff like that. I'm not even sure when I fell asleep.

At two in the morning, I woke to Kestrel's alarm, gathered my wits for a minute, and sent an inquiry to Twilight.

Not sick, she sent back, her thoughts quick and irritated.

I woke up just a little bit more. Twilight might not be sick, but something was up; she didn't sound remotely sleepy. Was she still trying to break out of her corral? Or maybe she really was feeling sick and didn't want to admit it.

Instead of taking her word for her health, I braved the cold and darted outside, groggy and yawning, and if truth be told, maybe complaining a little too. At the corral, Twilight trotted away from my flashlight beam, her ears back and tail swishing. Obviously, not sick. However, the trampled snow on her side of the gate showed me she'd been trying to escape for hours. I almost felt sorry for her – but then it was kind of her choice to get so frustrated. She didn't have to keep trying to get out. Instead, she could have saved her energy for all the bratty things that she wanted to do tomorrow.

Rusty nickered and meandered toward me, and I reached through the fence poles to stroke his furry face. His drowsy peace was welcome after Twilight's agitation. I reached to rub under his chin and he groaned, stretched his head out and closed his eyes in rapture. He was such a great guy. I was so lucky to have one horse that wasn't weird. Well, not weird if you overlooked his sleeping outside when he had a perfectly good shelter. It was way below freezing outside. My fingers were already stiffening up – but then I didn't have three inches of hair insulating my entire body either.

I gave my buddy a pat goodnight, shone my light on Twilight to see that she still appeared too upset to say hi to me, and then ran back across the yard. James hardly moved as I clattered up the porch steps, and then I was back inside the house. I threw some wood in the stove so the house would stay warm, then crawled back into my sleeping bag in the living room. Kestrel was snoring on the other couch, but it didn't keep me awake for long.

I dreamed of racing Rusty through the sparkling snow. White crystals flew around us, unique and glittering. And warm. So wonderfully, toasty warm. Then the rumble started.

My first dream thought: what has Twilight done now?

Sudden, raw excitement shot through my body. Thunder boomed in my ears and the ground shook beneath me. Dark shapes flashed past in a massive blur. James was barking somewhere, but I could barely hear him above the noise. What was happening?

I spun away to run – and fell off my couch, my sleeping bag a tangle around me. And yet the dream continued. Fearful excitement still poured through my body, the rumble still sounding around me, slightly muted now, but definitely still there.

Was this more than a dream?

"Kestrel?" I couldn't find the zipper for my sleeping bag. "Kestrel!"

"Mmpff."

"Wake up." I wormed out of my cloth cocoon, then crawled the couple of feet to her couch and clutched her shoulder. "Something's wrong. Something's happening outside. The horses..." I gulped. Was my first dream thought accurate? Had Twilight finally succeeded in escaping her corral and then done something terrible?

"What?" The couch creaked as Kestrel rolled over, away from me. "The bluebird... mumble mumble mumble… in the attic."

"Something's happening outside!" I yelled.

28

"What?" she asked a little louder, like maybe she meant it a little bit. "What's happening?"

"Can't you hear that noise?" I asked, still trying to collect myself. The first real bit of reason speared my mind; how could Twilight cause that?

"Zone into horses," Kestrel murmured.

Okay, so I'm not the most brilliant when I'm jolted awake in the early morning hours. I followed Kestrel's excellent and obvious advice and zoned into Rusty's vision as Kestrel fought her way out of her sleeping bag.

A dark river flowed by on the other side of his corral bars. No, not a river. Animals. Lots of animals. Then I recognized an individual shape. A cow. So Twilight *could* have caused this if she got out of her corral and opened the pasture gate. Suddenly, I felt sick. If anything happened to one of the cows, how would I ever pay Kestrel's family back? Each cow was worth hundreds of dollars, and that wasn't even counting the unborn calf each was carrying.

"What do you see?" Kestrel asked sleepily.

"The cows are out. They're running around the ranch yard."

"The cows!" Kestrel shrieked. Drowsiness gone! I had her attention now. She was right behind me as I stumbled toward the door and then struggled with my winter coat and boots. The mittens and other stuff could wait. We had to get the cows safe and under control, and then Twilight was *so* going to pay for this!

Kestrel was ready a millisecond faster than I was and jerked the door open. We tumbled onto the porch.

Dark cow shapes milled around the yard, snorting and stomping and lowing. I looked toward their pasture but couldn't see anything in the night.

Luck was with us. The moon chose that moment to peek out from behind a cloud. The ranch yard brightened to an icy glow. The meager light glanced off the red fur of more than a hundred nervous Herefords, dwelled on the whites of their eyes, lingered on the puffs of mist that were their breath. Over their backs, I could see Rusty *and* Twilight peering through the poles of their corral and almost collapsed with relief. For once, my mischievous filly was innocent.

"We have to shut the gate!" Kestrel yelled beside me. "Come on, James!"

I looked toward the pasture again, then realized that Kestrel was running in the opposite direction, toward the main ranch gate.

Oh no! We hadn't shut it before going to bed. Without a word, I raced after Kestrel – just as a bunch of about ten cows made a break for the gate, their bellies wobbling and hooves churning. Another ten or so streamed after them. They were going to beat Kestrel to the gate!

My friend screamed a command to James and he shot toward them like a large fuzzy cannonball.

"Go, James, go!" I yelled after him, then shut my mouth. Not smart to distract him. The race would be close as it was. Too close.

And then the lead renegade cows were through the opening, the others stampeding behind them. James was still struggling to catch them as they disappeared into the night.

Too late Kestrel and I reached the wooden bars. We stood in the cold, listening and hopeful and shivering as we waited for James to bring them back – but when his barking faded into the night, we knew he hadn't been able to turn them. Together, we closed the gate so no more cows could make a dramatic exit, and then gazed over the wooden rails at the tracks dimpling the moonlit snow outside the ranch yard.

Kestrel sighed and shook her head. "Looks like we're going on a cow hunt," she said morosely.

"Great." Meaning, *not* great. Meaning, why didn't we think to shut the gate last night? Meaning, this was really going to suck, tromping around in the snow for half a day looking for a bunch of ornery Herefords. No, not great at all. Not even a little bit.

Chapter 3

Five minutes later, Kestrel and I emerged from the house yet again, this time puffy with winter clothing. I'd taken the time to shove the last of the cookies into my pocket too. It was probably all the breakfast we'd get. However, we shouldn't be hungry for long – surely we'd have the stampeded cattle home in time for lunch.

James was slinking back when we walked out onto the porch, looking depressed and beaten, the poor guy. He'd done his best but the cows had been intent on escaping and he hadn't been able to stop them. We clattered down the steps as he rolled over in the snow and waited for his punishment.

Kestrel bent to give him a belly rub. "It's okay, buddy. You did your best." He stared hopefully into her eyes. She was forgiving him when he had so obviously failed? I gave him a pet too, just to reassure him a bit more, but he was obviously more worried about Kestrel's forgiveness than mine.

"So what do we do first?" I asked. Kestrel was the cow expert, not me.

"We find out how the cows got out," she said, straightening.

A sick feeling sprouted in my stomach.

"If it's something easy to fix, then we fix it and put them back in their pasture," Kestrel continued. "And if we can't fix it, we put them in the barn, then go find the others and bring them home."

"Okay," I said, hoping I didn't sound too guilty. This could all be my fault. Maybe I hadn't closed the gate properly when we'd finished feeding the cows, or I might have damaged the latch by hitting it with a rock – and here I'd first blamed Twilight for everything, when all she'd done was *wish* she could get into mischief.

Rusty and Twilight hung their faces through the fence and watched us hustle toward the cow pasture. The metal gate shone silver in the moonlight as we approached. And it wasn't askew. It wasn't open. The bars glimmered horizontally from gate post to gate post. Relief made me sag. I hadn't ruined everything with one whack of a rock. I hadn't put a whole bunch of cow lives in jeopardy.

But if the gate was fine, how did the cows get out? I scanned the moonlit enclosure. "I don't get it."

"Me either. Where did they…" When Kestrel fell silent, I noticed she was staring to the left of the gate. Her mittened hand crept over her mouth and she shone her flashlight on the destruction. "Oh no."

"Wow." An entire section of fencing was missing. Poles had been flung and scattered like sticks, and the snow around them was trampled and dirtied. Quickly, I worked out what must have happened; for some reason, the cows wanted to leave their pasture but couldn't because the gate blocked their escape route. So they pushed on it. However, since there were too many cows to fit along the span of the gate, some spilled to the sides and pushed on the fence – and the wooden fence obviously couldn't take all those heavy bodies leaning on it. It had collapsed and the cows had stampeded through like water poured through a broken dam.

"Why would they push like that?" I asked, stopping beside a pole that had been tossed more than fifteen feet from the gap in the fence. "Twilight was in her corral. She couldn't have scared them." A silly thing to add maybe, but Kestrel might not have noticed my filly hanging out exactly where she should.

James growled beside me and glared off toward the trees at the back of the pasture.

Fear prickles engulfed my body, making me quiver beneath my warm winter clothes. "I wish he hadn't done that."

Kestrel shone her light into the pasture to reveal nothing, then said something that I liked even less. "I wonder if they were scared by the bear. Even just smelling it could make them push on the fence."

James barked, his ruff rose, and he trotted through the gap in the fence. Kestrel called him and he reluctantly stopped as we both backed away.

"But he probably went back to his den," I said. I *really* didn't want it to be the grizzly. They were terrifying creatures with their massive muscular bodies and the humps on their backs and their long dirty claws and sharp yellow teeth, not to mention their horrible roars and how fast they could run.

"Maybe. We don't know for sure," said Kestrel.

"Even if it was him, he couldn't have been too close," I said, trying to balance my fear with a bit of reason. "I mean, if he had been, the cows wouldn't have stopped in the ranch yard."

"Some of them didn't stop."

"Yeah, but some of your cows are just weird. It's like they want to be wild or something."

Thankfully, Kestrel nodded. "Yeah, some of them don't like people much." Then, not the sort to mope over spilt milk or stampeded cattle, she spun around.

"Even if the grizzly is hanging around, the main herd should be safe in the barn while we get the others."

"So job one, put the *good* cows in the barn," I said.

We jogged back to the ranch yard, and minutes later, Twitchy was tied by the house, the main barn doors were wide open, and we were tossing hay into the arena from the loft, hoping to lure the cows inside. Having bottomless pits for stomachs, it didn't take much luring. By the time we had tossed about thirty broken bales over the edge, most of the cows were munching peacefully and James was nipping at the heels of the last few who seemed reluctant to enter the dark barn.

A few minutes later and Twitchy and Rusty were saddled and Kestrel and I were aboard. Light was barely touching the sky behind us, making us all glow like pale ghosts in the dawn. Soon the sun would be up, blasting down on us, or blasting as much as it could in mid-winter, and we'd be able to see the trail to follow it quickly.

Twilight pranced before us as we headed out, her head high and ears swiveling in all directions, thinking this was outrageous fun. She gave an extra little hop and twist when we opened the ranch yard gate.

Track cows? I asked as we followed her. We'd be able to go a lot faster if we could just follow an energetic Twilight. Her delight at being asked to do something she actually enjoyed sparkled inside my heart and she arched her neck and flicked her tail, proud as can be. I couldn't help myself; I smiled. She was too cute.

Kestrel asked Twitchy to trot, Rusty picked up his pace, and the three of us entered the forest on the other side of the snowy road. I was glad to get moving. Already, I was feeling chilled, and hopefully, trotting would make my muscles work harder and I could warm up.

We trotted and loped the horses as much as the trail would allow for an hour and didn't see a single cow, just a lot of cow tracks and some cow poo. We didn't even hear them, they were so far ahead.

When their tracks veered off the main trail, Kestrel and I slowed to a jog. I was still hopeful that they weren't too far ahead. Sure, my initial idea, that we'd be back to Kestrel's ranch in an hour or so, obviously wasn't going to happen, but three or four hours chasing cows wasn't the end of the world. When we got them home, we'd need a couple hours more to patch the fence, clean out the barn, and feed the cows, but we'd have both the time and energy for another fun filled evening.

The forest became darker, thicker, as the trees clustered closer together, but Twilight still kept up a steady jog, winding through the trunks like a pro. Rusty and Twitchy slowed to a walk, but I wasn't complaining. They were doing their jobs: keeping our knees away from tree trunks. I thought of asking Twilight to wait for us but then changed my mind. Now that full daylight had arrived, we could follow the tracks as quickly with her gone, and it would be nice if she could tell me how far the herd was ahead of us.

Another half hour of fast walking and occasionally trotting and still no cows, plus Twilight was almost beyond my hearing range and she hadn't caught up to them. I didn't understand it. Why was the herd still moving so quickly? Did they somehow know we were behind them?

We entered an unbelievably thick grove of trees, and the first thought that leapt to mind was worry for the super pregnant cows. I hoped none of them were with the escapees. If they had travelled through this thicket of trunks, they might have bumped their ballooned sides on the tree trunks as they squeezed through the tight spots, harming their unborn calves. The idea made me nauseous.

Bear!

My heart lurched and I pitched forward on Rusty's neck to cling for dear life. But before I was able to control the fear thundering through my veins, Twilight herself calmed.

Stump, she said.

I scowled and straightened shakily in the saddle, then glanced at Kestrel. Thankfully, she'd been too busy ducking beneath some low branches and hadn't noticed my weird actions.

We rode steadily for *another* hour, still not seeing or hearing a single cow. We were obviously on their trail because the snow was wrecked in front of us, mashed into dirty slush. But there were no cows to be seen. Very weird.

"So what's your mom going to do about getting a new agent?" asked Kestrel.

A strange thing to ask, I thought, but then I realized she might need something to distract her from worrying about the herd. I certainly did. "I'm not sure. Maybe advertise? Or go to Vancouver to find a new art agent to represent her paintings? It shouldn't be too hard, now that we know her paintings are famous."

"Wouldn't it be great if you could go with her?"

I smiled. That would be so beyond amazing.

"And if you have any time alone while you're there, you can do some investigating about her past and stuff."

"I'd love that so much. Maybe I'd even find out *why* she's hiding in the bush, or who started that website that's asking for information about her." I wrinkled my nose. "That still kind of creeps me out."

"Me too," Kestrel said. "But it would be so great to find all the answers. And bonus, after you can write a book about your trip and the mystery getting solved and everything, and make tons of money."

I couldn't stop myself from laughing out loud. "No one will buy a book about a trip to Vancouver."

"*I* would. But first of all, you need to make sure you get to go with her. I think she might try to leave you behind with us."

"Oh my gosh. You're right. She'd totally leave me behind without a second thought." I felt like smacking myself in the head. That would be *sooo* Mom. "But what can I do to make her take me?"

Kestrel frowned. "I don't know. Yet. We should think of some options."

And so we brainstormed some ideas which ranged from the totally ridiculous, like stowing away in Mom's suitcase, to the even more bizarre, like telling Cocoa to not let her in the saddle until she promised to take me with her. As if Cocoa would listen to me over Mom. Ha! Not much was accomplished during our thinking session, other than keeping us from worrying about the cows, but I'm pretty sure that's what Kestrel's goal was anyway.

I knew Twilight had stopped to graze near a swamp but was still surprised when we caught up to her. I guess that showed how much ground we were covering, even though we were keeping to a fast walk.

The sense of satisfaction that came from my filly as she filled her stomach felt so good that I knew my own body needed food. I still didn't feel too hungry because of all the excitement and activity, but it *was* already past mid-morning – which sucked, by the way. It meant my estimate of being home by lunchtime was way off. Even if we found the cows in the next hour we still wouldn't get them back to Kestrel's until afternoon.

"You hungry?" I asked Kestrel.

Kestrel looked back at me. "Am I hungry?" She raised an eyebrow. "I'm starving. Why?"

"You want some cookies?"

"Oh my gosh! You're my hero." Kestrel pulled Twitchy to a quick halt and I moved Rusty alongside her to hand her two cookies.

"Thanks."

The horses began to walk again, side by side. Kestrel took a bite and chewed methodically as she stared down at the tracks. "Why haven't we caught up to them yet?" she asked in a cookie-muffled voice.

"I don't know. It seems strange they haven't slowed down enough for us to catch them." I took a big bite of my first cookie, and my mouth seriously thought it had just landed in heaven.

"Do you think something's happened to them?"

Uh oh. I could hear a touch of despair in her voice. "No, no," I said quickly, spraying cookie crumbs. "They're going to be fine."

"But what if they're not? That would be so awful, and totally my fault too."

"No way. How can it be your fault? There's no way *anyone* will think it's your fault."

There was a long pause and then Kestrel spoke in a rush. "But Evy, what if one of them dies? What if one loses a calf? That'd be the worst thing, if a cow or calf dies when I'm supposed to be keeping them safe. Maybe no one else would blame me but *I* would."

I needed to get Kestrel thinking about something else. But what? The upcoming trip to Vancouver and my mom's mysteries had been analyzed to death, and I couldn't think of anything else good enough to distract her.

In front of us, Twilight stepped onto some boggy ground that for some reason hadn't frozen, and sank up to her knees. Of course, the cows had sensed it wasn't safe to walk there and had avoided it. Not Twilight. But she was more surprised and dirtied than she was in any danger – and I was glad for the distraction. I had no idea what to say to make Kestrel feel better.

Twilight climbed out of the mud just as we caught up to her, and she looked at us sheepishly. Then her expression changed and she put on a blast of speed to remind us that we belonged behind her. Freezing mud clots flew around us, little muck missiles, and Kestrel looked mad enough to shoot my thoughtless filly – an expression I liked a lot better on her face than despair.

"We'll just have to make sure that all the cows are kept safe," I said, trying to sound both confident and determined at the same time.

There was a pause, then, "You're right. We just do everything we can."

I could have kissed Twilight for helping Kestrel out of her funk, mud and all. Instead, I popped the last bite of my second cookie in my mouth to find a large clump of mud had attached to it. As I spit it out, my stomach complained like a wild beast denied its dinner. The morsel didn't go to waste though. It wasn't on the ground for more than a quarter of a second before it

40

was in James' stomach. The collie looked up at me and grinned before continuing on.

Twilight's tracks dirtied the snow for quite a ways and I think that's why we didn't see the blood sooner, but eventually Twilight lost most of her mud and we noticed the first spot of red in the snow.

Kestrel gasped and her hand rose to her throat as she stared along the trail of droplets. James ranged around us, then stopped short to sniff at the spray in the snow.

"Maybe it's just a scrape," I said quickly. "Those tree trunks were pretty close together back there. It would be easy for a cow to rub against the bark."

Kestrel looked at me, hopefully. "A scrape wouldn't be too bad." Then she gulped and her face became white. "Unless it banged up the baby inside her."

"That couldn't happen, could it?" I asked, even though I'd been thinking the same thing just a short while ago. "I think her body would protect it."

"It happened to a cow we had a couple of years ago," she said, her voice flat.

There wasn't much I could say in response, so I didn't say anything. From then on, every time I glanced at Kestrel, she was either leaning forward in her saddle and staring into the distance with a haunted, worried face, or looking down at the blood.

We followed the trail for another half hour, not seeing anything more than normal gross cow deposits – well, except for the blood, that wasn't normal. And it wasn't normal that they *still* hadn't stopped to rest.

Then we found out why.

Twilight stopped ahead of us, her head high and her ears straining forward so hard that her ear tips trembled.

Bear!

41

My heart revved into action. *Where?*

Rusty stopped short; I held onto the saddle horn and concentrated on information gathering instead of panicking. Bear smell filled my nostrils – or actually Twilight's nostrils, but it felt like mine.

Twitchy bumped into Rusty's rear. She'd been on autopilot, just following Rusty, and Kestrel must've been staring at the snow. "What's wrong?" she asked.

James growled.

"Twilight smells bear."

"I knew it," Kestrel moaned.

"It may have just accidentally crossed their trail," I said. Most of the time, grizzlies are kind of live-and-let-live creatures, with an "I eat my bugs and you leave me alone or I'll swat you" way of thinking.

"Admit it, Evy," said Kestrel, sounding exasperated. "Only a bear or a pack of wolves could have scared the herd so much that they'd break down their fence. Only the fear of a big predator would keep them moving so fast."

But I didn't want to admit it. The idea that the grizzly's presence here was no accident was too scary. It meant the bear was hunting – and a hunting bear was terrifyingly unstoppable. Kestrel and I would have better luck trying to stop a train.

"After we left this morning, it probably hung out around the ranch yard," Kestrel continued. "Trying to get to the cows in the barn."

I sighed and finally gave in. "Yeah, okay. You're probably right."

"Then when it was too hard to get to them, it decided to catch up to these ones, and now it's between us and these cows," Kestrel added in a chilled voice. We watched as Twilight stepped on top of the bear's tracks, following them back the way they'd come. James trailed behind her, leaping from track to track in the deep snow. They turned back at a clump of bony aspen. "It must have cut cross country and then picked up the trail here," she added.

"Not good." Actually it was a lot worse than not good. I'd clearly misjudged the bear's intelligence. He was much smarter than I first thought – maybe not smart enough to still be hibernating, but smart enough to get between us and Kestrel's cows by taking a shortcut. "What do we do now?"

Kestrel just shook her head. She seemed completely at a loss.

"We have to get around it somehow," I said, stating the obvious. "And then herd the cows to safety."

"Any ideas on how to do that?" Kestrel asked. I wasn't sure if she was being sarcastic or not, but considering the situation, probably not.

"We could take a shortcut too. We just have to figure out where the cows are going, and get there first." When Kestrel didn't say anything, I continued, "If a bear was after me, I'd go somewhere I felt safe. Maybe the cows are doing the same thing."

"Like home?"

"You think they're looping around and returning home?"

Kestrel's forehead crinkled. "No. They already think they're not safe there, and besides, we're getting close to the far side of Sparrow Lake. They'd have to turn around to get back, and if the bear's behind them, they won't turn around."

"So do they have a backup safe place on the other side of Sparrow Lake?"

"I don't think so."

"But they're the ones that picked this direction. They had to have a reason," I said, trying to get her to think. We had to find a way to save them and I didn't know Kestrel's range land the way she did.

"This is the trail to the catch pens, that's all," she said, dispirited. Then she inhaled sharply. "But maybe *they* think of the catch pens as being a safe place. We have a salt lick there in the summer," she added, sounding as though she'd just won the lottery. "Plus they love hanging out at the edge of the lake. Some of the cows truly hate it when we herd them back to the ranch for the winter. They keep trying to turn around."

"And there's a shortcut to the catch pens?"

"Yes! It'll be tough going, but if we cut across Marble Swamp, we can make it."

"All right, so that's what we'll do. Then we'll wait for the cows at the catch pens, herd them back across Marble Swamp ahead of the bear, and get them home and inside the barn where they'll be safe too."

"Awesome." Kestrel reined Twitchy to the left. "Let's get going." James trotted loyally behind her.

I mind-called Twilight. My filly was a touch reluctant to leave her investigation of the bear scent but still she galloped to catch us, and then pass us. After a few strides, Kestrel looked back at me. "Sorry to be so weird, Evy. I'm just worried, that's all."

"I know. But don't, okay? Worry, I mean. You can be weird all you want." My joke didn't even get a smile. "We'll get them home safe," I added.

Kestrel nodded and turned back around. She asked Twitchy to pick up the pace when we broke out into an open area and the mare moved into a tired trot, plowing her way through the untouched snow. James leapt from track to track at her heels.

I was happy to see Kestrel trying to be more positive. Now if only she wouldn't think what I was thinking – or at least not yet.

Bears could move fast if they wanted, much faster than short legged, pregnant cows. We had to find the herd soon and get them moving home, injured cow or not. The longer we were involved in this chase, the closer the bear would get to them – until it was so close there'd be no leaving him behind. There'd be no saving the slowest cow.

Front row seats to a grizzly bringing down a valuable Hereford? No, thank you. That was the last thing I wanted. We had to find them soon. No, sooner than soon. And then we had to hightail it home as fast as our horses' legs could carry us!

Chapter 4

The corrals at the salt lick were deserted. Untouched snow topped the fence posts with little cone triangles, gathered in drifts around the small cabin, and spread in riffles across the open areas. It was pristine and gorgeous, and I would've given almost anything to see the chaos of cow bodies trampling everything.

"Dad stays in the cabin when he comes out to check the cows in summer," Kestrel explained absently as we rode past the log structure. I didn't remind her that I already knew that. I preferred her acting like a tour guide to obsessing about cattle-hunting grizzlies. I only wished I could do the same.

"So which direction will they probably come from?" I asked.

Kestrel pointed away from the lake to the far end of the meadow.

"Should we go meet them?"

"Good idea."

The snow became deeper the farther we got from the lake, thanks to the open ground and the wind that blew most of the snow off the frozen water. Everything was gorgeous and winter wonderland-ish and made me wish circumstances were different. I wanted to laugh at Twilight's cavorting instead of worrying about rampaging grizzlies. I wished I could leap from Rusty's back to make snow angels. And the idyllic scene around us didn't remotely compare to the summers on this side of Sparrow Lake. I'd been here a few times before with Kestrel and had been blown away by the wildflower meadows, strung together like jewels in a necklace. Now they looked like milky opals on a white-gold chain. In summer, a blue, green, and purple mountain, now a sparkling white, hovered above us. There were little bubbling brooks meandering here and there, now frozen as hard as stone beneath the snow.

Just out of sight of the lake, we entered a meadow where two summers before we'd watched a mama deer and her twin fawns as they played for an hour, leaping and spinning about on their spindly legs. It had been beyond adorable, and I would've given almost anything to be back at that moment instead of stuck in this one.

I wasn't the only one on edge either. Rusty was on high alert. He was acting calm and responsible, the perfect saddle horse, but energy buzzed below his skin.

Twilight, of course, didn't even bother acting calm. She kept charging back and forth, sending snow spray over us every couple of minutes as she dashed from one intriguing thing to smell or see to the next intriguing thing. Then she perked her ears here, there and everywhere, chased James a bit, and finally galloped out of sight to see what was around the corner. I kept tuned into her perceptions but other than a mad jay and some cross squirrels, she didn't find any other living creatures. Which in one way was awesome. If the renegade grizzly had given up, I'd be ecstatic. The problem was that the cows hadn't shown up either.

"Do you think we guessed right?" Kestrel asked after we'd ridden for ten minutes and still hadn't seen any sign of the herd.

"Maybe they left the bear behind and then slowed down."

She looked at me doubtfully. "I know you're just trying to make me feel better, Evy" she said. "But don't, okay?"

"I'm just trying to look on the bright side," I said defensively.

"There isn't a bright side. One cow is already hurt and bleeding, and the bear's probably right behind them. He might've even caught one by now," Kestrel said, tears in her voice.

"Sorry, Kestrel," I said, quickly backtracking. Clearly, now wasn't the time for a lecture on the benefits of optimism. I had to remember to look at this from her point of view.

"I'm sorry too," she said, her words clipped in her effort not to cry.

Then the most beautiful sound came to my ears. A moo. Kestrel's face lit up like the sun. "They're coming! They made it!"

"Told you not to worry," I said, before I could stop my tongue. But Kestrel didn't seem to care. She was just happy to hear the cows. "Let's go check them out," I added in a steady voice, not wanting to sound too optimistic or positive or anything.

The first white-faced cow came into view. She trotted along quickly with her head lowered and her mouth open as she inhaled deeply. She was one of the not-so-pregnant cows, so she didn't sway too much as she pushed her way through the snow. Then she saw us and stopped. Her eyes widened and we could see the white rings around her eyeballs as she thought about running for it. Then another red and white, steaming cow came up behind her, and another and another. The front cow calmed as her herd mates joined her. More cattle crowded into view.

"Cow cows!" Kestrel called, like she does when she feeds them.

It was as if she'd caused an explosion. The herd surged toward us, suddenly bawling like babies, their dreams of independent living obviously long gone now that a dangerous grizzly was on their trail.

James started to bark and run in circles.

"Lead them toward the corrals and I'll count them as they pass," I shouted to Kestrel. She nodded and spun Twitchy away. James rushed after her, and as they loped off he kept looking worriedly over his shoulder, as if he was afraid the advancing horde would trample him.

"One, two, three..."

Cows here.

Four, five...

Yes, I told Twilight, and kept counting as the herd of almost identical Herefords continued to hurtle past me. There were small variations in markings, size, and stage of pregnancy but that was all, and they tended to run together into a reddish brown blur.

Six, seven, eight...

One cow shoved another aside, making the first cow do a nose dive into a snow bank. It came up with white powder dusting its surprised face and coning the top of its head like a snow hat. I couldn't help but laugh. More cows streamed past.

Nine, ten, eleven, twelve... or was that fourteen? Or even fifteen?

They were moving so fast. Because they wanted food from Kestrel?

Okay, so clearly I still didn't want to *completely* accept the grizzly scenario. *Bear?* I asked Twilight. She'd be able to tell me if it were near.

49

No.

I drew in a deep breath. Sixteen, seventeen, eighteen...

Suddenly, I felt Twilight on the move again. I sent out an inquiry and discovered that she was going to see if the bear was following the cattle trail. So what had her last *no* meant? The bear just hadn't been right exactly in front of her at the time? My shoulders locked with tension again.

Nineteen, twenty, twenty-one, twenty-two. Okay, so I'd miscounted, unless there were more than twenty escapees to begin with. I guess it had only been an estimate anyway. Probably the only way we'd know they were all safe was if the bear showed up; he wouldn't keep chasing the others if he already had his dinner. I *really* didn't want him to show up – shudder – but at least if he did, we'd know he hadn't brought down a cow. Yet.

I turned Rusty to follow the last of the swiftly trotting herd. Next item of business. Which cow was leaving its blood in the snow?

But there was no blood. Uh oh. Had the cow been left behind?

Hurt cow.

Through Twilight's eyes, I saw the injured cow grow nearer, but not because she was moving toward my filly. Instead, Twilight trotted toward the thrashing beast as the cow struggled to rise to her hooves.

"Kestrel!" I bellowed at the top of my lungs. "I need help!" She just had to hear me – even though she was out of sight now, along with most of the herd. There wasn't time to ride to get her, not with a hunting grizzly possibly scant minutes away. "Kestrel!" I screamed again.

No response. There was only one thing to do. Ask Rusty to gallop toward Twilight and the injured cow. Maybe the horses and I could rescue her alone.

We careened into the forest at the back of our meadow, along the wide trail, and finally broke into the last meadow in the chain.

Twilight stood at the far end, attentively watching the forest. I couldn't see the cow but as Rusty and I moved steadily toward Twilight, the prone creature came into view. My first thought was gratitude. She was one of the smaller cows. Her belly didn't look like an extended balloon about to pop at any moment. My second thought: this cow was in *serious* trouble. She was lying on a slope and her hooves were uphill of her body. It was going to take a lot of strength for her to get up.

She froze when she first saw us, then redoubled her efforts to rise. Her hooves scrambled on the slippery slope and seemed to catch! She heaved her front half up onto her trembling legs, then positioned her hind legs beneath her. Pushed up! And thumped back down, panting.

"Kestrel!" I tried again, though by now I was too far away for sure. I just didn't know what else to do. Rusty and I looked down at the poor cow. This was the injured one, all right. Blood marked the snow beneath her back leg, though not as much as I would have expected. Maybe the cold snow packing against the wound was helping it. Or maybe I was just trying to be positive again.

I looked back along our tracks. Still no Kestrel. We were going to have to do this without her, somehow. I slid from Rusty's saddle and waded through the snow around the cow in case I'd missed anything from my higher vantage point. She didn't take her white-rimmed eyes off of me as I pushed my way through the knee-high fluff, almost twisting her neck into a knot.

"It's okay, cow," I said, in case a soothing voice would calm her.

The cow shuddered, totally un-soothed, and lurched forward. Another mighty attempt to rise, and once again, she *almost* got there. And this time, because I was on the ground beside her, I saw exactly why she couldn't get up. She did fine until she needed to use her left back leg, the injured leg, to rise. Even if the slope she was on wasn't so slippery, she still wouldn't be able to get up. Her hurt leg just wasn't strong enough anymore.

And I saw the cause of all the blood. The culprit was a stick, a sharp, strong stick, about two inches across. There was nothing unusual or extraordinary about it, except that it stuck out from her hindquarters like a short spear. She must have run into it in the forest and impaled herself, and then broken it from the tree as she kept running. Poor thing. Every time she fell back down, she would feel terrible pain – and falling back was all she'd ever be able to do. She didn't have a snowball's chance in July of getting up on her own with the injured leg on the downhill side and her hooves uphill of her body.

Somehow I controlled the soft soothing words that fought to fall from my mouth, knowing they would only freak her out more. But I was going to end up terrifying her anyway. I had to get close to her, even touch her, if I was going to save her.

The way I saw it, I had two options. The next time she tried to stand, I could rush to her injured side and push to give her some support. Since she could almost make it on her own, my light body weight pushing might be enough to help her rise completely. The down side of that plan was that if she did fall back again, she could land on me.

The second option seemed even harder; roll her over so her hooves were downhill and her uninjured leg was the main one she'd need to stand. Then she could rise herself. *But* that would require me to stand at her side, right where her hooves would be striking and flashing, to push her over. Way too dangerous.

As if wanting to test out my first scenario, the cow once more lurched forward and strained to straighten her now shaking front legs beneath her. I could tell even as she started that this wasn't as strong an attempt as the last two. She must be weakening with each effort. Probably the only reason she was trying at all was because I was right beside her, but better me than the grizzly. He certainly wouldn't help her get up.

When her front legs were stable, she started to slip, slide, and scramble her back feet beneath her again. It was hard, watching her and wanting to help but having to wait for the perfect moment to rush in. Too soon and she'd probably slip and fall as she tried to get away from me with panicked, spastic movements. Too late and she'd already be falling back and there'd be no way my meager strength would stop her. All I'd do is get squished. I had to rush when she was almost up, when I could give her that momentary shove at the pinnacle of her rising and then she could propel herself forward, probably limping dreadfully, but still on all four hooves.

I waited for lingering seconds as she tried and tried and tried to get the injured leg to push up beneath her – all it seemed to want to do was shake – and then her eyes rolled back in her head and she sank down. A loud "oof" exploded through the winter air when the end of the stick hit the snow and was probably driven a little deeper. Harsh. I wanted to cry as I looked at her. The poor thing didn't have much strength left. Unless she rolled over and got her good leg beneath her, I could see no hope for her.

Unless, I could somehow *pull* her over. Maybe...

But to do that, I needed a rope. I didn't have a rope.

Rusty tossed his head up and down, his dark mane a jumble of long hair above his endearing face. His bit jingled in his mouth.

Bella – I was tired of calling her "the injured cow" – groaned. The low sound was full of misery.

Rusty shook his head and his bit jingled again. *Pull over*, he said.

No rope.

This time Rusty vigorously swung his head from side to side, and finally I understood. He was suggesting I use his bridle as a rope. The reins were long and split, and that's what we needed to help Bella. Lots of strong rope-like material.

Great idea, I thought to him as I moved back around Bella. I pulled the headstall over his ears and he opened his mouth to let the bit fall, then I unhooked one rein from the bit and tied it to the end of the other rein to make a longer rope. I made a loop in the end of my new "rope" as Rusty and I moved around to Bella's downhill side. Not the kind of loop that tightens when it's pulled. The last thing I needed was for the leather to tighten around Bella's leg and then for her to get up and walk off with Rusty's bridle dragging behind her. I needed a loop that would stay the same size, not so big that it would slip off her leg, but big enough that it would slide over her hoof and past her knee once I had it on her.

And that was going to be the first hard thing to do, get it on her leg. At first I tossed it a few times, just in case I got a lucky shot, but all that happened was that the loop landed in the snow and on Bella's big stomach and every other place I didn't want it to go. When I finally realized I needed to put it on manually, I tramped around to stand between her head and forelegs, though not so close that she could strike or butt me. I took a deep breath and reeaaacchhed out with the loop, while Bella glared at me like she wanted to kill me.

And just as I touched the tip of her hoof, she flung both front legs forward and tried again to lurch to all fours. I sprawled backward in the snow, attempting to get away from her sharp hooves, and watched her fight to rise for another few seconds before she thudded back to earth. Still and panting and once again consumed by the pain of her injury, Bella lay with stiff legs, moaning. This was my chance! I flung myself out of the snow, rushed forward to grab her hoof, and shoved the loop over it. Her healthy back leg took a swipe at me, but only succeeded in brushing my leg. It was enough to make me gasp as I limped the few steps around behind her again, but not make me stop.

Finally on the downhill side of her, I pulled on the reins. The noose slid up her leg, just as I'd hoped, snagging on her knee – but as she fought the feel of the leather around her leg, it slid past her knobby joint. Success! Now I just had to pull her over.

Bear!

Twilight's sudden terror hit me like a fist and I sank to my knees in the snow as my eyes wildly sought the beast. And there it was.

Oh my gosh! I could see it with my *own* eyes!

A furry mountain loped toward us, a mountain with a cavernous mouth and jagged teeth and huge muscles and scimitar claws.

I couldn't help it. I screamed. And I can't tell you how anyone or anything reacted to that awkward cry because my eyes were full of one thing and one thing only. A grizzly with hunger alight in his eyes swiftly closing on us. A grizzly completely intent on me, Bella, and Rusty.

Chapter 5

I wanted to run. Believe me, it wasn't bravery that kept me rooted to the spot. No, it was total and complete fear. Something bumped my arm, hard, but I really wasn't into noticing much more than the behemoth with slavering jaws and daggers for claws that galloped toward us.

The bridle was jerked from my hand as the cow saw the grizzly and tried again to rise. Tried, and didn't succeed.

Rusty hit my arm again. *Must go!*

And then Twilight was between us and the grizzly. Dancing. There was no other way to describe it. Her neck was arched and her black mane tossed like a dark wave as she pranced and leapt with a buoyant bounce just a couple of feet out of his reach. Her tail switched side to side as if in time to music. My brave and snarky little horse was trying to save us by distracting the grizzly long enough for us to make our escape.

I hurried to Rusty and was about to climb into the saddle when Bella gave a loud bawl behind me. I looked back long enough to see her give a super-cow effort to stand – and I just couldn't abandon her to her fate.

If luck was with us, this would just take a couple seconds. I'd already done the hard part, getting the rope on her leg. I rushed back to her, grabbed the bridle from the snow, locked my mittened hands around the end of the rein and pulled with all my strength. Luckily, I pulled just as she was about to try lurching to her feet again. My force knocked her off balance and she thudded down on her back. I scrambled backward in the snow, trying to keep the rein tight, trying to pull and all the while wondering, what on earth was I doing? There was a grizzly just yards away, and Twilight could only keep him occupied for so long.

And then I was dodging slashing cow hooves as Bella rolled the rest of the way over and her hooves fought for purchase on the slippery slope.

I didn't waste any time. I raced to Rusty's side. Forget the bridle. There was no way I was waiting for the rein to come loose from Bella's foreleg so I could collect it. Time to get out of here!

Safe in Rusty's saddle, I looked for the bear and Twilight – just in time to see the horrendously vicious beast make a rush for my filly. She dodged his raking claws with an inch to spare, and I almost cried out again.

Rusty jumped forward, and I noticed that Bella was up, staggering in the direction of the lake.

Make her move faster, I said to Rusty. If we wanted to help Twilight, we had to get out of here. I knew my stubborn filly. There's no way she'd leave the bear if we were still vulnerable. But I also knew she wasn't being totally selfless. Last fall Twilight had been so disappointed when the grizzly had chased everyone but her. Finally her wish had come true. She certainly had the grizzly's full attention now.

Bella tottered and swayed up the slight slope – then slipped. No! But she only went down as far as her knees and then she was up and hurrying onward.

I turned in the saddle to see what was happening behind us just as the bear made another short rush at Twilight. She barely kept ahead of him and, thinking

58

he'd taught her a lesson, he turned back to us. Big mistake. Suddenly, she was right in his face with her shaking mane and snapping teeth and flashing hooves. He swatted at her, obviously surprised, and she took the opportunity to dash behind him and bite his bottom. He spun around, roaring, but... too slow. She was not only well out of reach but was flinging a saucy look his way. I smiled as I looked back over my shoulder. It was kind of fun watching Twilight use her amazing pest talent to infuriate someone besides me.

Bella stopped for a moment, closed her eyes, and swayed side to side. "Move it, slowpoke," I said, none too gently, and she looked back at me with scared, angry eyes, then moaned, and stumbled onward.

When I looked back again, Twilight and the bear were even farther from us, and not just because we were moving away from them. She was slowly leading him toward the back of the meadow. Then we entered the trees and I couldn't see my filly anymore.

Be careful. He only has to touch you once to hurt you. I sounded just like Mom that time, even to myself, but I was so worried.

Twilight didn't respond. I reassured myself that she must be concentrating on the grizzly, that she was too agile to be caught, that she was much too smart, and then firmly pushed the *too arrogant* out of my head. She just had to be okay.

Rusty jogged along as quickly as Bella could hobble, and we moved through the chain of meadows, farther and farther from Twilight and her pursuer. I felt as if my heart had been left behind and kept tuned to my filly's experiences as she dodged the bear, teased him, further enraged him.

"Evy!" Kestrel sounded so far away.

59

I didn't have the loud voice that Kestrel did, so I pushed Bella into a faster limp – and the noose I'd fashioned from Rusty's bridle finally fell from her front leg. I made a quick retrieval and was back in the saddle before Bella had a chance to rest, then as Rusty kept her moving, I tried making the bridle useful again with my stiff, cold fingers. My efforts were useless. His bridle needed a lot more repair than what I could give it while riding.

As I hung it on the saddle horn, Twilight's thoughts flowed into my mind, quieter now that she was getting farther away. *Bear coming!* I zoned into her vision to see the bear's bum as he stalked away from her. Had he finally given up on catching her?

Then his bum got closer. Twilight was making one last effort to distract him. Quietly, she snuck up behind him, then reached out, teeth at the ready.

The bear roared and spun, paw swinging, and nicked Twilight's muzzle! She wheeled away, shaking her head and sending droplets flying, then raced for the trees.

My heart felt like it was hammering its way out of my chest as the bear rushed after my filly, his tiny bit of success giving him hope.

Twilight reached the trees and sped beneath their cover, then glanced back to see the bear barreling after her like a freight train, knocking saplings aside and mowing down bushes. Had she ever succeeded in her task! The bear was so angry that she was all he could think of right now. Good for us, but not so good for Twilight if she slipped, or stepped in a hole, or came to a log too big to jump over...

Please, please, be careful, I told my filly even though she doesn't believe in being careful. Obviously.

Twilight sent me a feeling of reassurance. She was fine. Don't worry. She could handle this bear. Her last thoughts were like whispers. She was almost out of range.

Rusty and I pushed Bella into the meadow at the edge of Sparrow Lake to see Kestrel waving to us from the middle of the mooing cattle herd. She yelled something that sounded like, "Stupid cows!" and motioned to me to come help her. Leaving Bella to make her own way to the herd, I asked Rusty to gallop toward my friend. As I drew near, I realized she was inside the corral along with most of the cows. Why?

Kestrel waved her arms and yelled at the hefty beasts but they hardly seemed to notice her. James skulked around the outside of the corral, clearly at a loss regarding what to do with the loud and extremely stubborn animals.

Kestrel and I met at the corral fence. "What's with these cows?" she asked, sounding desperate. "They're acting totally stupid. They barged into this corral and won't leave."

"Maybe they think the fence will keep them safe if the grizzly comes," I shouted back.

Kestrel's face became a degree paler. "We have to get them moving before it gets here. But they're not listening to me."

"It'll be harder to ignore two of us," I yelled, and turned Rusty toward the open gate. Dumb cows, thinking this thin rail fence could protect them from a grizzly. Of course, they'd just break it down if the bear appeared, just as they had last time, but by then it would be too late. The bear would be sure to nab at least one of them and probably injure more than one.

I glanced back along our trail as Rusty pushed through the cows near the gate. Bella had almost reached us. And she wasn't slowing down now that she was near the rest of her buddies. Did that mean something? Had the grizzly realized he'd never catch Twilight?

I sent out a question to my filly but she was gone. She had to be out of range. I wouldn't accept the other reason for her silence. My amazing and brave filly had to be okay.

Twilight?

Still nothing.

"What's wrong, Evy?"

A shudder travelled through my body from my head to my toes. "Nothing, she's fine," I said in a strong voice, trying to counterbalance the fear that must have been visible on my face.

"She? What are you talking about? What happened?"

I didn't answer Kestrel's question, because I couldn't. Emotion was abruptly choking off my throat. So instead I opted for action. *Must move cows now*, I said to Rusty, trying to concentrate on the job at hand. *Bear might be coming.*

Rusty almost unseated me by his wild leap into action, shoving his way through the crowd at the gate, biting cow butts and backs, and throwing me from side to side in the saddle. The herd scattered outward, clearing the gate. I clung to the saddle horn with both hands as my gelding moved farther into the corral, pushing this one, shouldering that one, and biting all the rest. He was a dynamo, a cow-saving terror. I looked up once to see Kestrel staring at us, her eyes round with shock, but most of the time I just concentrated on hanging on for dear life. Last thing I wanted was to tumble from

Rusty's back and end up as an area rug to a herd of sharp-hooved cows.

When most of the cows were out of the corral and the rest were looking at us with a lot more respect in their white-rimmed eyes, Kestrel, Twitchy, and James entered the fray. A minute later, the corral was empty. We stopped at the gate, all five of us breathing heavily.

"Remind me never to make him mad," said Kestrel, looking down at my wonderful gelding.

I just laughed – a little shakily. I was just thinking the same thing. I gave Rusty a pat on the shoulder. *Thanks*.

He snorted and bobbed his head. No time for thanks. There were things to do.

"Twilight's going to be okay, Evy," Kestrel said in a quiet voice.

Tears threatened. I nodded, still unable to speak my fears aloud, plus infinitely glad that Kestrel was such an understanding friend that I didn't have to. My gaze raked the back of the meadow. I almost hoped to see the grizzly. If he showed up, it meant he hadn't gotten Twilight and she was just off somewhere, doing Twilighty things.

"We should get going. It's going to be dark soon," Kestrel said.

Sure enough, the sun was close to the far horizon. Uh oh. "We won't be home before dark if we go back across Marble Swamp."

"I know."

"So you think we should..." I stopped. The idea of crossing the lake on the ice was kind of scary.

"I can't think of a better plan," said Kestrel.

"What about along the lakeshore?"

"It's still too far, and besides, we'd have to break trail, so it would still take hours."

"You think the ice will be thick enough?"

"There are only a few cows, and it's already December," Kestrel said, shrugging.

A few cows that weighed thousands of pounds altogether. Ice that first froze up less than two months ago. "You're the expert," I said to my friend, and took a deep breath. She was the one who knew these ranching things, not me. And besides, by the time it got dark I wanted to be sitting in a nice warm house and eating a massive meal, not riding through frozen, crowded forests in the dark chasing a bunch of skittish, brainless cattle and eluding a prowling grizzly. "Before we go, we should help Bella," I suggested, trying to take my mind off the ice crossing. "That's the hurt cow. She has a big stick jabbed in her leg."

"You named her?"

"Yeah, and I should have named her Grumpy, not Bella. Wait until I tell you what happened in the meadow." Kestrel looked at me, expectantly. "Tonight," I added. "We have to hurry now."

"So which one is she?"

"Uh," was all I could think to say. Brilliant, I know, but really, they all looked the same.

"Let's ride around and see if we can find her."

"Sure." I closed the gate to the corral in case the cows decided to go back inside, then we rode through the tired herd, looking for Bella.

I glanced again toward the back of the meadow. Still no sign of the grizzly. James barked from the other side of the milling herd and Kestrel rushed toward him. Then she waved to me. They'd found the cow.

The herd parted like water as Rusty and I approached. A minute later, we were on both sides of Bella, pinning her between us so she couldn't move sideways. She tried to shake us by lurching forward, but we just moved along with her. After a minute she stopped and Kestrel leaned down from Twitchy's saddle to take a closer look at the wound. She reached down to touch the stick – and the second her fingers made contact, Bella bawled and kicked out hard with her injured leg, then she staggered forward again.

Kestrel looked worried. "We need to get her home where we can pin her down. There's medicine there too."

I nodded. "You go first and I'll push them from behind."

Kestrel and Twitchy walked toward the lake. Following my thought instructions, Rusty moved behind the cows, and I started to yell and wave my arms. The cows, still nervous of us – okay, nervous of Rusty – trotted after Kestrel and Twitchy. Then they reached the ice.

It wasn't slick ice, having a thin layer of snow sticking to it, but it was enough to unnerve the cows. Rusty pushed and I yelled and James entered the fray with his sharp bark and sharper nips, and finally the brave lead cow stepped out onto the ice. The others followed her carefully, and then Kestrel and Twitchy trotted off again, leading the way. So far, so good.

The herd bunched together as they moved farther out onto the ice. The lead cow started to jog and the others kept right up to her. They weren't going as fast as Kestrel and were slowly falling behind, but I was still happy. They weren't leaving Rusty and me too far behind either, and we could only go as fast as Bella.

The offending stick still dripped the occasional blood drop as she tottered forward. Her pale pink tongue hung from her mouth as she panted for air and she looked as though she was using her last bits of strength to keep going. But she was still going. I was impressed, and even though she was incredibly ornery, I didn't want to push her too hard. She'd just had the worst day ever and was in pain, exhausted, hungry, and terrified. Except for the pain thing, I knew exactly how she felt. On top of all the stress and fear my stomach felt like it was glued to my backbone.

I sent my horse-radar out again to Twilight, just to check. Still no answer.

The main herd packed tighter together in front of us. From above, the cows would look like the solid point of an exclamation mark moving across the ice. Then I noticed we were gaining on them.

No, Bella hadn't gotten faster. They were slowing down.

Then they stopped.

Bella stopped too, and I loped Rusty around her. What did they think they were doing, having a rest break? There'd be no breaks until we got home. The sun was sinking closer to the horizon every minute; the worst kind of deadline.

Rusty slipped on the ice and I asked him to slow to a walk. That's when I noticed the trembling. Huh? And even weirder, it felt different than it would if he were cold or hyper. It was like the tremors were travelling up his legs.

A loud snick of cracking ice sounded around us. Rusty's forelegs slid a couple inches toward the cows.

Oh my gosh! The weight of the herd was making the ice sag. It couldn't handle the twenty plus cows, all jammed together, and was sinking beneath them!

In the middle of the herd, a fountain erupted into the air, spraying high. Water was escaping the pressure of the sinking ice by shooting through the cracks. I knew what would happen next: the entire chunk would give way and the entire herd would be dumped into the lake.

We'd never get any of the cows out if that happened. We didn't have any ropes with us to pull them out. They wouldn't be able to climb over the broken edge of the ice because they were exhausted and pregnant and wouldn't be able to grip the ice with their hard hooves. Nor would they last long in the water. Within minutes, their bodies would start shutting down because of the intense cold and they'd just sink out of sight. Or worse: float on the surface, dead as buoyant doorknobs. Both possibilities made me nauseous. This was beyond terrible. It was – it was unacceptable.

Kestrel raced Twitchy over the ice, back toward the herd. But what could she do?

Whatever it was, I should do it first. The cows were closer to me.

But what could I do?

And suddenly, I knew. The weight of the combined cows was causing the ice to buckle, not the weight of the individual cows. I had to split them up before the section gave way completely.

"Let's go, Rusty!" I yelled and sent him mental instructions – his bridle was still hanging on the saddle horn, so I couldn't use that – and to his credit, my loyal gelding leapt forward. Moments later, he was in the herd, biting and kicking and scrambling on the super slick surface. I yelled and waved one arm, my other hand firmly clutching the saddle horn.

The cows on the edge scattered, slipping up the slight incline, but the others crowded closer to the epicenter of their demise, trying to avoid their equine attacker. But there was no avoiding Rusty. One by one, the cows were sent scrambling up the slippery slope they'd created – and then Rusty and I reached the lowest part of the sinking ice. Freezing rain fell around us from the pressure fountain as Rusty bit and slipped and struck out like a maniac. I hung on and yelled at cows and prayed that the ice wouldn't give way while we were in the danger zone, and the cows ran from my wonderful Rusty like they'd never run from the bear.

At one point, I saw Kestrel on the edge of the water, looking at us with a horrified face.

"Keep them moving!" I screamed to her, just in case the cows continued to be stupid and bunched together somewhere else.

She started to yell something back to me – and then Rusty slipped, crashing down hard on his right side and pinning my foot beneath him. Pain blinded me and somewhere, far away, I heard Kestrel scream.

I tried to jerk my foot free and horrendous, jagged pain screamed through my leg, up my body, and through my mouth. Desperate, I tried again. My elbow slipped and my right side splashed into the freezing water pooling on the slick surface. My head smacked against the ice, hard, and I gasped in a mouthful of icy liquid. Gagging. Choking. Stars spinning.

I had to escape!

Chapter 6

I fought for a handhold in the ice, a crack, a bump, anything to grab so I could free my leg. The water was sooo cold. My teeth clanged together so hard, that I knew if my tongue got between them, it would be a goner. My clothes soaked up water like a sponge.

Then Rusty's calmness touched me. First it skirted around the edges of my panic, but slowly, gently, it infused me. Even lying on his side on ice in six inches of freezing water with glacial rain splashing around us and the ice about to give way beneath us, he was still taking care of me.

Hold on.

I grabbed enough reason to do as he said, clutching the icicles that were his mane with my wet mittens and holding on as tightly as my near-frozen fingers could manage.

My friend and confidant, my most trusted ally in the whole world, gently positioned his body so I'd be able to stay aboard, and carefully rose to stand.

Out of the water, I panted and wheezed a bit, then gingerly reached down my leg to where it had been pinned and poked it. It wasn't hurting nearly as badly now with Rusty's weight off of it. In fact, I could hardly feel it. I wasn't sure if that was a good thing or not.

"Are you okay, Evy?"

"I... I think so," I croaked. "But I'm soaked."

Kestrel knew the gravity of those words as well as I did. I was at serious risk from hypothermia. "We need to get you home fast."

"Start moving the cows," I said through chattering teeth. "We'll get the last ones to follow." If we could just get moving, at least Rusty would warm up.

Kestrel nodded and Rusty and I turned back to the cows left in the hole, now standing ankle-deep in water and staring at us like we were monsters. And Rusty was pretty monstrous for the next minute. By the time the last cow left the sunken watery pit, we were all soaked. Kestrel still hadn't moved the herd toward the ranch but as soon as Rusty and I were on safe ice, she called the cows and headed out. For once, the hairy beasts organized themselves in an even line as they followed her. Maybe they were just too tired to act dumb anymore.

Rusty and I settled in behind Bella and pushed her to hurry as my clothes froze on my body. The temperature dropped as the sun slid down the sky and I felt so cold I hurt all over. In an hour or two, it would be below freezing and I didn't know what I'd do then. At least right now, I was still shivering. You're only really in trouble if you stop shivering, if you stop feeling the chill.

To be safe, I needed to stop and light a fire but that was impossible. Though I always carried matches with me as a safety thing, they'd be soaked and useless now. And besides, what could we burn in the middle of the lake? I would keep warmer if I ran beside Rusty, but I knew I wouldn't be able to keep up with the herd. I didn't have any feeling left in my feet anymore and would be falling all the time. No, my best chance of survival was to flex my trembling muscles and flap my arms to create body heat as we trotted along, and get back to the ranch as soon as possible. After a minute of this, I realized my spastic movements had a bonus benefit too; they kept Bella moving.

The dark line of trees at the edge of the lake grew steadily nearer as the sun sank lower. When the last bit of light was sucked behind the distant hills, we finally reached the edge of the ice. It was chewed to bits by the cows that had gone before us, and water sloshed in a narrow trough against the shore. Rusty leapt over it, almost unseating me, and then *tried* to move carefully up the bank, which meant he did a number of short lurches instead of one massive upward plunge.

The ranch was as close to the lake as I remembered, but still, the fifteen minutes it took to ride there seemed like fifteen hours.

Rusty, Bella, and I reached the ranch gates just as Kestrel was hurrying toward them. Countless cows ambled about the yard behind her. She must have let the main herd out of the barn for some fresh air before coming to meet us.

"There you are," my friend said, relief alive in her voice. She moved aside so we could enter the ranch yard and shut the gate behind us. Then, suddenly, she was at my knee. "Are you okay, Evy?"

"I look that bad?" I croaked, surprised that my voice was so rough.

"No, of course not," she said and looked down at the snow.

Okay, so clearly I looked terrible. Well, no surprise, I felt terrible too. The only part of me that was warm was my teeth, which felt on fire from the pain of clanging together for an hour. I tried to wrap my mittened hand around the saddle horn so I could swing my leg over Rusty's back and dismount, but my fingers wouldn't grip. In fact, I couldn't even feel them anymore.

"Actually, you're covered with ice. You look like the abominable snowman."

"Thanks," I managed to say.

"Just slide off. I'll catch you." She grinned apologetically at me as she held out her arms. "I won't tell anyone."

Yes, it was embarrassing, but really I had no choice. I tipped sideways and Kestrel was right there to catch me – but of course, I was too heavy and she fell backwards and we both ended up in a heap in the snow. Kestrel struggled to her feet, then pulled me upright. I tried to smile in gratitude but my face wouldn't move.

"Can you go into the house and stoke up the fire?" asked Kestrel, plainly giving me a way to keep my dignity and get warm at the same time. "We're going to need the heat as soon as we're finished with the cows."

"I can help you with them first," I said, being stubborn, though I don't know why. All I wanted was to go inside and wrap myself around the stove.

A line appeared between Kestrel's eyes. I could almost see her thinking of another excuse to get me inside the house. Then her expression lightened. "Okay, but go change your clothes first. You can't move very fast when everything's frozen."

I sighed, resigned, and reached for Rusty's reins before I remembered he wasn't wearing his bridle. And it wasn't on the saddle horn anymore either. Great.

"I'll take care of him and Twitchy together. It'll be easier that way," said Kestrel, though she didn't explain how taking care of two horses was easier than one.

"But..."

Kestrel reached for Rusty's forelock so she could lead him. "Evy, go get warmed up," she said, looking me right in my eyes.

Surely I wasn't as bad off as what she thought. I was still moving. Kind of.

"*Now*," Kestrel added, suddenly sounding a lot like her mom.

I tried to shrug. There was no use arguing when she sounded like that. Instead, I turned toward the house. If I hurried, I could be out to help her in just a minute or two.

The problem was that I couldn't hurry. No matter how good my intentions, it took forever just to get to the house. Turning the doorknob was a marathon and then when I was finally inside and the warmth that still lingered in the house washed over the exposed skin on my face, all I wanted to do was sink down and sleep.

However, I forced myself to be tough. It was dark in the house so I felt my way to the cupboard where the kerosene lamps were kept. I pulled my mittens off with my teeth, and then felt for matches on the counter. Sliding the box open was almost impossible, but I got it open by tipping the box and shaking it. Then I tried to light a match. Big joke. I couldn't even hold onto it. The slender wood kept slipping from my unfeeling fingers and then when I tried to pick up the matches in the dark, I couldn't even tell if I was touching them. I took more and more from the box, and then just dropped them too.

Finally I gave up and worked on removing my thawing jacket. No luck in undoing my zipper. My hands really were useless.

I went into the living room and opened the stove door, then threw in some wood. That I *could* do. No fine movements required there. The wood landed on top of the coals and moments later, the first lick of flame wrapped around the wood. I shut the door and opened the flue, then went back to the kitchen again to try lighting the lantern.

Okay, so that's enough detail. Suffice it to say that by the time I had given up on lighting the lantern, had found the wind-up flashlight in the cupboard near the door, removed my saturated clothing and put on some dry clothes from my backpack, it seemed as if a lot of time had passed. My hands were no longer numb. They burned as blood returned to my swollen, still-clumsy fingers. I threw some more wood in the fire, shut the flue down a bit and then started looking for another coat so I could go back outside to help Kestrel. I found a warm ratty coat covered with hay seeds in the closet by the door, plus some boots that were a couple sizes too big for me. On the shelf inside the closet, I found a thick scarf, a wool hat, and two mismatched mittens to wear.

As I reached to open the door, I heard a distant thought.

My human?

Huge relief made me whimper. Twilight was alive! And she had to be close to the ranch if I could hear her.

We are here, I answered. *You okay?* I didn't wait for her to respond but started scanning her sensations – and I could feel no pain from her. She was not only alive but seemed unscathed, except for the nick on her muzzle that I already knew about. She was, however, bone tired.

Back soon, she reassured me.

So glad! I couldn't stop myself from smiling. My brilliant filly was almost home and she was safe, and this after she'd not only saved Rusty, Bella, and me, but had clearly outsmarted the renegade grizzly. Hopefully now he was on his way back to his den, having finally accepted that there were no free dinners at this ranch.

When I stepped outside, I was shocked at how dark it had gotten. Full blown night had arrived. The cows were dark shapes wandering about the ranch yard. I turned on my flashlight and threaded my way through the herd to the barn. Kestrel was probably inside, already trying to help Bella.

The barn was gross; the stay-at-home cows mustn't have done anything but eat and poop all day. I found Kestrel inside, staring over one of the stall doors that lined the back of the large arena in the barn. James was beside her, panting heavily and looking like he'd just exerted a lot of energy.

"I'm glad you brought a light," Kestrel said. "I can't see anything but I'm pretty sure James chased her in here." I wound the flashlight for a moment, then held it high. Bella was indeed in the stall, standing against the far wall and staring at us with angry eyes, as if she was positive the stick still protruding from her back leg was our fault. A deep, lowing sound rumbled toward us and she shook her head.

"You feel strong enough to help me pull the stick out?"

"Sure. But should we? It's not bleeding anymore," I said. "If we pull it out..." Terror shot through my body. A monstrous shape loomed over me and I spun away, screamed and felt air blast against me as the dark shape struck.

And missed.

"Evy! Evy!"

Kestrel's alarmed cry called me back to my own world and I found myself on the dirty floor of the barn. "Just a sec," I gasped as I fought to push Twilight's terror out of my mind. My filly's blood seemed to pound through my head, through my muscles. Her heartbeat echoed in my bones. I didn't need to ask her what had happened. I knew it as well as if it had happened to me.

Twilight had been walking the trail back to the ranch, more tired than she'd ever been in her life and yet feeling safe, believing she'd finally shaken the grizzly, when he'd lunged out of the darkness before her, teeth snapping and claws slashing. Only her fine-tuned mustang reactions had saved her; she had automatically sprung backward, turned tail and run.

I felt myself calm a little as she galloped farther through the snow, wildly searching over her shoulder for the giant bear.

Run home, fast! But on different trail, I called to her, and felt her agreement. A detour would take a few extra minutes, but she'd probably still get here before the bear.

Before the bear...

Yes, he would be coming. Our ordeal wasn't over yet.

"Evy, talk to me! What's wrong?"

I groaned. Kestrel wouldn't want to hear this news but she had to know. We had to get ready and fast. "The grizzly," I said, "he's coming."

"He can't be. We left him behind," Kestrel said with all the fervor of someone wishing something horribly true was just a bad practical joke. "He wouldn't come all the way back here."

"He would. He just tried to nab Twilight, and she's nearby."

"Yeah, but..." But what more could she say? If the bear was coming, he was just coming. Arguing wouldn't change anything. "Twilight's okay?" she asked.

"Yeah," I said, grateful I'd told her about my ability to understand horses last fall. Now would've been a terrible time to explain it. "She's running back here. He'll be close behind her, so we need to get the cows in the barn right away."

"If we throw down some hay, they'll come inside quick for their supper."

"Good idea. Then we can shut them inside. I just hope..."

"What?"

How I hated always bringing up bad stuff. "I hope the grizzly doesn't feel like ripping the doors open."

Kestrel looked sick. "They aren't as strong as the rest of the barn." Then her face brightened. "The lights! We could turn on the lights!" she yelled, her fear making her a lot louder than normal.

"Great idea." That should keep him away, or at least it would keep a normal bear away.

"I'll go turn on the generator and you start throwing hay down into the main part of the barn," said Kestrel, and then she was hurrying away from me through the dark.

"Take the flashlight!" I called after her, tracking her form with the beam.

"Are you sure?" she asked, turning.

"Yes. I can feel my way to the loft."

Kestrel came back and took the flashlight gratefully. "You'll have lights in just a minute. I'll flip the switch when I leave, and then when the generator turns on, the lights will come on in here."

"Turn off any lights in the house before you come back," I said as the flashlight beam retreated. "We want the generator to last a long time."

"Good idea." There was a click, the barn door opened a couple of feet, then closed behind Kestrel, leaving me in absolute darkness. For a moment, I couldn't move. It wasn't just the dark. I'd been in dark places before. It was the thought of that grizzly bear steadily lumbering nearer the ranch. Could he see the buildings yet? Could he hear the tired lowing of the cattle?

Would one of them die tonight?

Sudden anger infused me. I'd had it with this bear. He'd terrorized us all day and now he was going to try the same into the night? Enough already!

I turned to my left, arm outstretched and wiggled my fingers in the air, searching for the loft ladder. Hadn't it been right here? Had I gotten turned around?

I heard something shuffle in the straw to my right. Bella?

I am here.

Rusty. He was inside the barn? But of course he was. Kestrel had said she was going to take care of him.

And Rusty could see in the dark, or at least he could see better than I could.

Ladder to hay?

Rusty snorted and a question filled his mind. He didn't know what I meant. Then in the distance, I heard a roar. The generator firing up. Light flooded the barn.

Rusty looked at me from his small stall and chewed the hay that Kestrel had given him. Twitchy was in the stall past his, her head buried deep in her manger.

Thanks, I said to my buddy, even though he hadn't had time to help me yet.

I glanced at Bella before hurrying toward the ladder to the loft, hoping that her expression looked softer in the full light. No such luck. I'm sure she would have pawed the ground and rammed the stall door with her thick head if she'd had more than three good legs. Maybe Killer fit her better than Grumpy. One thing was for sure, a pretty name like Bella certainly didn't suit her.

I climbed the ladder as quickly as I could with my beaten body. At least it would be easy to feed the cows this time. I just had to cut the strings and push the hay bales over the edge of the loft, letting them land in the arena.

In, said Twilight, and I paused to zone into her experience. She was at the ranch gates, the *closed* ranch gates.

Call Kestrel, I thought to her. My friend was already near the gates and could get to Twilight a lot faster than I could. I reached into my jacket pocket for my penknife. Oh yeah, this wasn't my coat. *Call loud*, I added, just in case Kestrel was already in the house, shutting off stray lights.

My eyes sought the twine cutter that I knew Kestrel's family kept in the loft. There it was, hanging on its hook near the top of the ladder. Seconds later, I slashed open my first bale, jerked the strings away, and pushed it over the edge.

After five bales, I was slowing down as a result of no food and spending an exhausting day in freezing temperatures. Maybe I could eat some hay or something. Ha! I wasn't that hungry yet. Oats sounded good though.

I heard a shrill squeak and looked down to see Kestrel pushing the big doors open. "Did you see Twilight?"

"No. Is she here?"

"She's at the gate," I said and started to descend the loft ladder. "She was supposed to call you."

"I might've been in the house. I grabbed some bread for us."

"You're my hero."

Kestrel grinned. We reached the stalls at the same time, and she shoved the plastic bag holding the bread into the empty stall. My stomach almost made me leap on it but somehow I controlled the inclination. Kestrel rushed to the hay I'd already thrown down and picked up an armful. I copied her, and together we hurried toward the big double doors. Time to lure the cows inside by creating a hay trail for them – and then I'd go get Twilight.

I dropped mine inside the door and Kestrel continued outside. "Cow cows!" she yelled. Then she was streaking back into the barn, a massive herd on her heels.

I pressed against the barn wall so I wouldn't be trampled. "Run, Kestrel!"

She dropped the hay and dove out of sight over the short wall that separated the stalls from the arena.

"Are you okay?" I yelled. "Kestrel?" Were we both going to survive this experience? Why had I been so eager for Mom to leave?

"Yeah, I'm okay," Kestrel said and her head and shoulders appeared over the half wall. "Hurry with Twilight, okay? The bear could be here any second."

"Okay."

I slipped through the big double doors and around the corner of the barn, not realizing until I stepped out of the light that I had forgotten the flashlight. I heard the soft crunch of snow and then something touched my mitten. "James?" I said hopefully, and the dog whined beside me. "Let's go get Twilight."

The stars lit the ranch yard with a soft silver glow that became brighter as my eyes adjusted. I peered ahead to the gate as I tromped through the snow, James at my side. There, to the side of the gate, a dark form.

Twilight?

Yes. No recriminations about being slow. No 'hurry up, hurry up.' Nothing but silence. My poor horse. She'd done so much today, so much more than any of us. She'd tracked the grizzly, herded cattle, been a brilliant decoy, even been slightly injured by the bear...

I opened the gate enough for Twilight to walk through and slid my hand along her side as she passed me. Icicles clung to her long winter hair and tinkled beneath my touch.

Bear near, Twilight said, her thoughts slow as molasses in my mind.

Come eat. There would be lots of time later to talk about the bear. Twilight needed to get her strength up.

My gallant filly trotted toward the barn and I closed the gate behind her. I knew it wouldn't keep a bear out, but it just seemed wrong to leave it open. Then, not questioning Twilight's quick pace when she was so obviously tired, I jogged after her. At the open barn doorway, she bit a couple cow butts, chasing the last two inside the barn, and entered behind them. At the door, I stopped and watched her push her way through cows to the biggest pile of hay.

Kestrel waved at me from the loft to get my attention. "Are they all in?"

81

"I'll check once more." Surely I had enough time. I stepped back into the night and waited for my eyes to re-adjust to the low light – but I was too close to the brightness streaming from the open doorway to tell for sure. With James at my side, I moved farther into the darkness. Slowly, so slowly, I started to see shapes. Fences. The house. The woodshed. In the distance, the metal gate to the cow's enclosure glimmered faintly as it caught residual light from the barn. No cow-shaped forms moved through the night.

A low rumble came from beside me.

"What is it, buddy?" I asked the collie. My mittened hand found his shaggy fur. "Do you see another cow?"

Then I noticed it too; a dark shadow blocking the shine of the metal gate. A large dark shadow.

Another pregnant cow?

Or the bear?

But wouldn't the bear follow Twilight's tracks to the front gate? Surely this shadow was a cow.

But then why was James backing away from it?

Suddenly, he barked a loud and high pitched yowl-yelp. My heart jumped in my chest as the shadow rushed toward us, silent, smooth, and swift – and moving unlike any cow I'd ever seen.

I ran.

"James! James!" I screamed at the dog, but there was no need to call him. In a flash, he was ahead of me, looking back over his shoulder as if the devil itself were after us. I didn't dare look back. I didn't want to know how close it was.

I reached the light spilling from the barn and felt like I'd just reached heaven. The bear had to be afraid of the light. I jerked on one massive door and swung it closed with a bang, then before I could chicken out, rushed back into the night to pull the second barn door shut.

I didn't need the light spilling from the barn to see what was waiting for me. I didn't need starlight. The grizzly stood on his two hind legs, his paws just feet from the brightened snow.

For the second time ever in my life I couldn't move, and as the massive tower of muscle and frustration and hunger glared down at me, I felt more frozen than when I was actually freezing to death. Then the bear's gaze slid past me to linger on the cows inside. A woof burst from his cavernous mouth, and he started to shrink. He was coming down onto all four paws.

That was all he'd do, I told myself. He wouldn't step forward. He was afraid of the light.

But still, the sooner I shut the door, the better.

It seemed such a simple thing to do. Grab a door. Pull it shut. But my body remained frozen. It was almost as if it had decided I was going to be Victim Number One. My feet were stuck in the snow, my hands glued to my side. My eyes locked on the bear as it landed on all four paws.

And then stepped toward me.

Chapter 7

Maybe my body realized it only had two choices: do something or be dinner. Maybe it finally grasped that this *was* a serious situation, I don't know. But finally my fingers wiggled – and then my hand shot out and scrambled along the massive wooden door, searching for a knot, a crack, anything to use to pull the door shut.

The bear took another step toward me and entered the light. Brightness glimmered from his tiny eyes, glanced off his long pale claws. Slowly, he pulled his lips back to reveal dirty, pointed daggers for teeth...

And then I touched the edge of the door. I wrapped my fingers around the frail wood, pulled, and stepped back. The door swung shut.

Somehow, I lifted the bar across the two doors, making them secure. Then trembling uncontrollably, I leaned back against the wood. A cow bumped into me but I hardly noticed and certainly didn't care. Not after the close-up of what was on the other side of the thin wood door.

Thin wood door!

I jumped away and spun to face it, half expecting the grizzly to come charging through. And I saw movement through the crack between the doors – a glistening eye. He was still there, watching us, waiting, deciding whether to break in or not.

"What's wrong?" Kestrel called. She was in the middle of the herd now, spreading hay around.

I backed away from the door, then my hands darted to my mouth. Had James made it inside? "James?" My voice was a thin croak.

Somehow Kestrel heard me. "He's by Twitchy's stall. Are you okay?" She hurried toward me. "What happened? Are they all in the barn?"

"I... uh... well... yeah, they're all in here." How could I answer her other questions? Kestrel appeared more relaxed than she'd looked all day, now that the cows were safe in the barn and she thought the bear was afraid of the lights. So much for that idea. Another massive shudder ripped through my body and I felt like puking. I bent and retched, but nothing came out.

"Come over here," said Kestrel, and I felt her hand on my shoulder. She directed me along the side wall to the back of the barn, then opened Rusty's stall door. I walked inside and collapsed against my wonderful gray gelding.

Bear outside doors. At least I could think the words.

Rusty put his ears back and snorted. Somewhere in the middle of the cattle herd, I felt Twilight perk up and listen.

"What happened out there, Evy?" Kestrel asked gently. "You have to tell me."

"The bear is out there," I whispered. "Right outside the door, just a few yards away. No, a few feet."

"You saw him? He wasn't afraid?"

I shook my head. "I mean yes, I saw him. And he didn't seem very afraid to me."

"What if he breaks down the door?"

"I don't know," I said, feeling another wave of nausea. We'd all be fair game then. Kestrel and the horses and I would be lucky if he just hurt one of the cows. And those doors? I had no illusions. They were

85

nothing to him. He could break those wooden doors like I could snap a couple of toothpicks. Our only hope was that *he* didn't know that.

"Well, he hasn't broken in yet," Kestrel said, suddenly being the optimistic one. "That has to be a good sign. The light must be *helping* to keep him away, at least."

I didn't say a word about how the only thing the light had done was shine on his long, curved claws as he stalked toward me.

Abruptly, Kestrel groaned. "Oh. We should have tried the radiophone before the bear got here."

My heart sank. Kestrel was right. We'd been so consumed with getting the cows to safety, we hadn't been thinking clearly. Or had we? The cows were our responsibility, and we'd only had a few minutes to act.

"If Mom and Dad were in their hotel room, they could've answered and then phoned the police or someone to send help," she continued.

"But we didn't have time. After we knew the bear was coming, we had to get the cows in the barn." There's nothing like trying to make your friend feel better to make you push your own fears aside. And besides, Kestrel was right about one thing. The bear hadn't broken down the door yet. Maybe he *was* a little bit afraid of the light, enough to not rip at doors with light shining out through cracks anyway.

"We should've assumed it was coming and phoned," Kestrel continued, sounding beyond miserable.

"We're doing the best we can, so let's not look back and second guess ourselves, okay?"

Tears filled Kestrel's eyes.

"It's going to be okay," I said, and forced my voice to sound calmer, more confident. "Plus I think we're doing awesome. That bear hasn't had his beef dinner yet."

Despite her tearful face, Kestrel laughed. "You make this all sound so civilized, Evy. Like he's going to dish up his plate and then eat with a fork and a knife."

"Don't forget the napkin tucked under his chin," I said, though he would look as terrifying whether he had a napkin beneath those sharp yellow teeth or not.

"We might need to tell him to keep his elbows off the table," she added.

"Bears don't have elbows," I said, even though technically I think they do.

Kestrel laughed again, a touch too loudly this time. I felt a bit hysterical too. Not good. We had to remain calm. Otherwise, we wouldn't stand a chance against this grizzly. All the brawn was on his side. Our only advantage was our brains and if we gave that over to thoughtless panic, well, we were toast.

And there in the stall beside us was the perfect distraction to frantic hysteria. Bella, or Grumpy, or Killer, whatever her name was. Actually, with a real killer just outside the doors, *Bella* sounded pretty good.

I suggested to Kestrel that we doctor the cow's injury and she clung to the idea like it was a lifeline. Without a doubt, she wanted something to keep her mind from the terror lurking outside too.

Together we left Rusty's stall and looked over Bella's door. And good thing we did. The poor thing no longer looked defiant, nor was she shaking her head at us. She was on her front knees with her big bum up in the air and her nose mashed into the straw as she tried to take some of her weight on her short face. Both of her hind legs were quivering as if an earthquake was underfoot.

Kestrel grabbed my arm and pulled me away. "Okay, so here's the plan," she whispered, all business once again. "She looks pretty out of it now, so I think we can sneak up on her. Then we give her a shove so she falls onto her good side."

"What if she hurts herself when she fights to get up?" I asked.

"We can't let her get up, so that means one of us jumps on her neck after she falls. The weight should hold her down," Kestrel continued. "Then the other one can pull the stick out. We'll have to watch out though, because she'll kick. We'll need some water too, and some clean rags from the feed shed to stop any blood flow."

"And then what? We sit on her all night?"

"We'll have to give her a shot too," said Kestrel, ignoring my silly question. "An antibiotic, in case there's infection. I think I know the right dose."

"What about a tranquilizer?"

"There's a bottle of that too, but I don't know how much to give her or if I should do the shot into a muscle or a vein."

"Okay, so skip the tranquilizer. You should pull out the stick and do the shot, since you know how to do that kind of stuff. I've never given a cow a shot before."

Kestrel shrugged. "Sure. But it's easy. It's just the same as giving one to a horse."

Apparently, she'd never tried giving a shot to Twilight.

A couple of minutes later, we were poised to enter Bella's stall with our clean towels, water, and a massive antibiotic needle.

Cow down, said Twilight, not meaning Bella.

What more could go wrong tonight?

Busy, I replied. Kestrel and I could handle only one cow disaster at a time here. Hopefully Twilight's cow was just tired and wanted to catch a few zees.

Kestrel opened Bella's stall door and we slipped inside, tiptoed through the straw until we were lined up along the cow's injured side – the sight of the stick jabbing out of her upper leg made me feel sick again – and then Kestrel yelled, "Now!"

We both jumped forward and rammed into the surprised cow. Bella tried to straighten her front legs so she could jump away, but she wasn't quick enough. She tumbled over, bawling and legs waving in the air. I landed on her side near her shoulder, then quick as the lash of a whip, rolled onto her neck and hung onto her head where her horns should've been as she pitched and shuddered and thrashed.

"You got her?" Kestrel yelled behind me.

"I hope so."

"Okay, here goes!"

I couldn't see what was happening, and yet I could tell when Kestrel pulled the stick out. Bella bawled, a queasy, wavering cry full of pain. I didn't dare risk turning to see the wound for fear that would give Bella some leverage to toss me off her neck. She was a lot stronger than I was.

"How does it look?" I asked.

"It's really gushing," Kestrel said breathlessly.

Cow panting, said Twilight. *Sick.*

Busy, I said again.

"Do we have enough towels to stop the flow?"

"I hope so."

Keep others from stepping on her? I asked Twilight. If we worked as a team, maybe we could save both cows.

Horsey sigh. *Yes.*

Thanks.

Minutes dragged past. I didn't want to tell Kestrel about the second sick cow until we had the first one treated, but it was taking sooo long for the bleeding to stop. Twilight kept sending me updates too and it didn't sound like her cow was getting any better. In fact, she seemed to be in more distress as time passed.

"It's still bleeding, but not much," Kestrel finally said. "Maybe another ten minutes and then I'll finish cleaning the wound and give her a shot. How does she look on your end?"

"Totally zoned."

"Really?" Kestrel said, dismayed. "Okay, let's wait five more minutes instead. We don't want her to go into shock from having someone sitting on her."

"Okay. And I hate to say it but there's another cow that needs help. Twilight's keeping the others away from her so she doesn't get trampled."

"Another cow down? Great. That's just what we need."

"It's going to be okay, Kestrel."

"Yeah." She didn't sound too convinced.

The five minutes we waited felt like thirty. Kestrel finished up, gave Bella the shot, then shoved the shot needle and all the bloody towels into the empty water bucket, and carried the bucket outside the stall. "Okay, let her up," she said from the doorway.

I jumped off Bella's neck and hustled to the stall door, worried she'd want revenge on me for being so mean to her – not that I was *really* being mean to her, but she might interpret it that way.

But there was no need. At the door, I turned. Bella was shakily climbing to her hooves. At first I wondered if she'd make it, but her good hind leg was on the correct side for her to stand and soon she was on all fours. Little shreds of straw fell from her side as she trembled. Then, as if to help us, she lurched to her water trough and gave us a good view of her injury as she drank.

Kestrel had cleaned it nicely and the hair around the puncture wound was wet with water, not blood. There wasn't even a tiny trickle of red.

"She doesn't look too bad," Kestrel said, both proud and relieved.

"She looks great. You did an awesome job." I smiled at her and she grinned back.

"Thanks. Now let's go see about that other troublemaker."

Okay, so this cow – I'll call her Marsha, for no reason whatsoever except that she looked like a Marsha to me – was flat on her side in the back corner, her legs out straight, and she was straining. Kestrel, the cow expert, saw the problem in a second. Marsha was having her calf early. She was one of the super pregnant cows, so it was probably okay if the calf was born tonight, but I still felt nervous. This time *two* lives were in our hands, both mama cow and calf – which, by the way, I immediately named Fred.

Marsha strained; Twilight, Kestrel, and I waited, and all the other cows ignored us as they gulped down the hay. Things stayed that way for a long time, or it seemed that way to me anyway. I didn't know what to do and Kestrel didn't see any need to assist when everything appeared to be progressing normally, so while Marsha did her thing I checked out Twilight's muzzle in detail. Just as I'd thought, the nick wasn't serious. It had hardly bled and wouldn't leave a scar. Lucky Twilight, once again avoiding injury. I didn't know how she did it, always putting herself in danger, and always coming out unscathed. She was simply and truly amazing.

The wall creaked right beside Marsha. Something was pushing on the outside of the barn, something large and strong. It didn't take a genius to know what was there, but just in case we hadn't guessed, the bear growled at us.

"He must smell her," whispered Kestrel.

Marsha rolled her eyes and gave a loud, mournful sigh.

"Can't we do something to hurry her up? Or maybe we should try to move her away from the wall?" I shifted a couple feet further from the wall myself. The wood, which had seemed moderately sturdy just moments ago, suddenly seemed far too thin.

However, there was no need to worry. Marsha took care of the problem herself. First, another exasperated sigh rumbled from her throat and then she lurched to her cloven hooves and staggered further into the herd. We followed right behind her and the herd enveloped us. I noticed that none of the cows moved close to the growling wall though. Maybe they were smarter than they looked.

A good thirty feet from the wall, Marsha sank to her knees, then rolled onto her side like a big cow balloon with a head and legs. She groaned, strained, and a white bump appeared beneath her tail.

From there on, things went really fast. Kestrel knew to open the placenta and to grab Fred's legs and pull at the same time that Marsha pushed. I helped her as much as I could but I don't know if either of us actually helped that much because Fred's forelegs were as slippery as wet eels. But someone did something right, because after a few pushes from Marsha and pulls from us, Fred lay on the ground behind his – oops, *her* – mom and gazed around with the cutest, biggest, longest-lashed eyes I've seen in my life.

Then she was up and down, up and down, splay legged and adorable, as she learned to walk. Kestrel and I laughed and shrieked as we tried to help her and got covered with birth goo for our troubles. Fred learned awfully quick and soon was jumping around in little baby jumps, running up to us and bunting us with her soft wet nose – and then Marsha finally decided it was time to get up. Our fun was over. Mama was back. Fred didn't mind though. She started to nurse and Kestrel and I stepped back so the two could bond.

The first calf of the year was always a cool event but this one had been super special. I was glad Fred was a heifer, a girl calf. That meant she'd probably join the herd when she got older and have babies of her own, rather than get shipped off to become hamburgers and steak. Life can be unfair sometimes, though I know that the steers on Kestrel's ranch, the male calves, are treated well until their time to contribute to human society.

"See? Everything's going to be okay," I said to Kestrel as we wandered back to the horses' stalls. Twilight followed us, stuffed with hay and very sleepy.

"Maybe."

"What do you mean, maybe? We saved an entire herd of cows from a grizzly today, plus helped an injured cow, plus just helped the world's most adorable calf be born. We can do anything."

Kestrel smiled. "Freda is cute."

"Freda?"

"Well, we can't call her Fred."

We stopped at Rusty's stall and I gave him a neck rub. Kestrel yawned beside me, and I couldn't stop myself from copying her. After the day we'd just had, I was ready for some sleep, and it even looked do-able now. Life had won over death yet again. The grizzly seemed to be staying outside. He could lurk about all he wanted, I didn't care, as long as he didn't intrude into our safe barn cocoon. The cows were relaxing too and a lot of them were lying down to rest, some even in the corner that had growled earlier. Their body heat made the inside of the barn toasty warm. It was a great end to the hardest day of my life. Time for some of that bread Kestrel brought from the house, and then maybe a snooze in the loft.

Then the distant engine roar hiccupped. The lights dimmed for a second, before brightening once again.

"The generator," Kestrel gasped.

"What's happening to it?"

"It's running out of gas."

My peace was shattered in an instant. In moments, we would all be plunged into darkness. Cows would be startled by the sudden night and rise to their hooves to rush about in an interior stampede. Not that they weren't used to the dark. They were. They just weren't used to it being bright as day one moment and then deepest darkest night the next. And it certainly didn't help that they could sense a grizzly nearby.

Next, the bear would be driven to distraction by the scent of their heavy bodies bumping about in the shadows and rubbing against the barn walls. I'd heard of grizzlies ripping doors off of pickup trucks just to get the lunch someone left inside on the seat, and these wooden doors were nothing compared to metal.

The generator roar sagged again and the lights dimmed for another long moment. I heard the bear growl before they brightened, and was too scared to note from which direction. But he sounded louder, more insistent, even eager.

A few cows climbed nervously to their hooves.

Soon the generator would die, the lights would go out, and the cows would panic. And once they started rushing about, mooing and shoving, what would happen?

I wished I didn't know the answer to this question.

Then, unless Kestrel and I could stop him, the bear would be upon us.

Chapter 8

"What are we going to do?" Kestrel whispered.

"I... I... let me think." But all my mind did was race to impossible things. Like if we had big lighthouse-sized lanterns that we could put around the barn, we might be okay. Or if we could just get our hands on a cannon, then we could scare the bear off. Or even better, fireworks. That way we could both scare him away and have something cool to look at as he ran.

The generator faltered, sputtered, hiccupped – and continued to run.

"We have one minute, max," Kestrel breathed beside me.

"Fires in front of the barn doors," I said, adjusting my lantern idea a bit. We had hay bales. They'd burn. As long as we had matches. My hand automatically flew to my pocket, but of course it was empty. I was wearing a borrowed coat.

"I have matches," said Kestrel, her hand in her pocket. "If they're not wet."

Please make them not be wet, I prayed as she pulled the worn box from her pocket. Trust Kestrel to carry matches too. But then it wasn't like it hadn't been drilled into both of our heads by our parents, who all had a thing for being prepared for every situation. Still, I doubt any of them had a rampaging grizzly on their minds when they'd insisted on matches and pocket knives.

Kestrel struck the first match to check if they weren't too wet to work. The flame flared and in that exact moment, the overhead lights went out, like a camera flash in reverse.

The lights came back on and the match died in Kestrel's hand. She reached for another.

"Wait. You don't have a lot. We should get the bale ready before you light anymore."

"Okay."

Moments later, Kestrel was up in the loft, tossing down unbroken bales. The cows crowded around the fresh hay until I waved my arms at them to shoo them away. Why didn't they go after all the loose stuff lying around? Instead, all they seemed to want to do was trample it now.

I dragged the first bale to the big double doors, being careful not to get too close to the boards that now seemed so frail. I mean, what if the bear's big paw broke through right when I reached the doors, then grabbed me and whipped me out into the night?

The generator stopped and darkness fell over us like a shroud.

The cows stomped nervously. A few mooed. One bumped me.

"Evy!"

"I'm here by the doors," I replied, pathetically trying to keep the dread out of my voice.

"Stay there. I have the flashlight."

Oh my gosh! The relief at knowing there would soon be a light, however meager, almost overwhelmed me.

"It's not working!" Kestrel wailed.

Terror spiked my heart. And then I remembered. "It's a wind up!" I shrieked.

"Oh, yeah." Seconds later, dim light cut through the absolute night, bobbed from up high to down low as Kestrel descended the ladder, then revealed the cows that thought they'd sneak a bit of hay from the bales Kestrel had thrown down. Caught in the act, they didn't even have the decency to look guilty.

"Point the light this way, so I can come help you," I called.

Kestrel shot the beam in the direction of my voice and I waved my arms and shoved my way straight into the milling herd. Twilight too was moving toward the bales. All three of us reached the hay at the same time and Twilight sent the last hay thief on her way with her eager snapping teeth. We swiftly pulled the last two bales across the dirt floor with Twilight following behind and making stay-back gestures at the cows.

At the double doors, Kestrel straightened and shone the light on the wood. She looked like she didn't want to open the doors any more than I did. What if the grizzly was standing there just as I'd last seen him, looking like a furry mountain with teeth and claws?

"Should we light it first and then drag it out?" Kestrel asked.

"But what if the fire gets too big before we get it all the way outside and we can't drag it anymore? The cows will really go nuts with a fire in the barn," I said.

"But what if we try to light it outside and it won't work?"

"Then we'd be outside with nothing to scare the bear away," I said, voice hushed. "Not what we want."

Kestrel looked at me with the same sick expression that I felt on my own face.

"Let's light it inside and drag it out," I said and clenched my teeth so hard that my jaw spasmed. It was risky but there was no way I wanted to open those doors to the night with only the spindly beam from the windup flashlight to protect us.

"Okay."

There was no need to loosen the hay in the first bale. The cows had already done that for us with their strong teeth. As I held the flashlight, Kestrel lit a match near a tuft sticking out of the bale. The match flared. The hay ignited. Kestrel moved on to a second tuft. When her match went out, she scooped a handful of trampled hay off the ground and held it to the flame, then moved the new fire to a third chunk of the bale.

The cows were noticing the fire and it was making them even more nervous. They were moving faster now, their white rimmed eyes bright in the firelight as they flashed past us. We had to hurry before they all-out panicked. I touched the rough lumber of the bar and lifted it, then put my hand on the door to push it open – and stopped.

"What's wrong?"

Good question. "Nothing. I'm okay." But still I couldn't seem to make myself open that door. I had Frozen Body Syndrome all over again.

"We need to hurry," encouraged Kestrel. "The fire's getting higher." When I didn't move, she asked, "You want to switch places? I can open the doors if you want."

Oh, how I wanted to switch places. But I knew I'd never live it down if I did. I'd always know I'd chickened out and my best friend had to cover for me, and I didn't want to live with that cowardly feeling for the rest of my life. "No, I'm fine," I said, took a deep breath, and pushed the door open with a mighty shove.

The flashlight beam cut the night.

Nothing! Or at least nothing for the narrow ten-foot length of snow that the flashlight illuminated. It would take the grizzly about a second to move that far. Or a half second. No, probably less.

"Hurry," Kestrel said behind me.

I stepped backwards. I wasn't about to turn my back on the bear if he was there, watching us. My back grew hot.

"Careful!"

I'd stepped on Kestrel's foot. "Sorry."

"You almost fell in the fire."

"Sorry."

"Just hurry, okay?"

I grabbed one of the two strings holding the bale together. Kestrel was right. We had to get the bale outside before the strings burned through. Otherwise, the neat package of hay would disintegrate into a burning heap and we'd have no way to move it any further.

When the bale hit the snow, even snow trampled by more than a hundred heavy animals, it slid faster. I kept my eyes turned to the darkness behind me as I leaned back, helping to pull the flaming bale along. This had better work. It really would be beyond horrific if the bear wasn't afraid of fire.

A cow bawled and Kestrel and I both straightened. She directed the flashlight beam to illuminate a lot of white faces, quickly heading our way. Then Twilight leapt between them and what they thought was their freedom. Dumb cows!

For a moment, I didn't know if my skinny little filly would be able to stop them. She was taller than the cows but certainly a lot lighter. If only Rusty wasn't locked in his stall, then he could help her.

But I should never have doubted Twilight. She not only foiled their escape toward the jaws of certain death, but she did it with style and a flip of her tail, making it look easy. Kestrel and I did our part, running toward the doors and pulling them shut behind us.

First mission accomplished; bear and burning bale outside, all cows, horses, humans, and dogs safe inside.

A thud came from the back of the building and a bear huff exploded from behind the barn. The cows went into a new frenzy. Dust rose into the air and I covered my mouth to stop myself from coughing.

"He's pushing at the walls, looking for a weak spot," said Kestrel, and though she'd said it loudly, I could barely hear her above the sound of trampling cows.

"Are there any weak spots?"

"Just the doors, I think," Kestrel answered, but she didn't sound overly confident.

"Good," I said, deciding to believe her words and not her tone. "So let's get more fires in front of the barn."

First, we opened the door to check the flaming bale. It was still burning fiercely, so we crept outside and threw on some scrap lumber that Kestrel found inside the barn. The flames rose higher into the night sky.

Second, we dragged the remaining two bales out through the big doors. By that time, the wood on the first bale had ignited, so Kestrel grabbed the unburned end of one short two-by-four and lit my way as I dragged the second bale nearer to the right front corner of the barn. Hurriedly, she lit it on fire. As the light spread across the snow, I peered into the edge of night. No bear, at least not close enough to see. Relief!

We hurried back to the third bale, and this time Kestrel pulled the bale and I lit the way as we moved it near the barn's left front corner. Again, we lit the hay on fire. Again, we searched the night. The growing blaze spread across the white expanse, lighting a circle

101

around us and making the dark appear even more impenetrable than before.

But still, I saw his movement.

"There he is," I whispered, and pointed along the side of the barn. The dark shape hunkered beside the wall, just a few yards from the last vestiges of light, a shadow blacker than the night. A low growl rumbled toward us and grabbed my heart, making it flutter like a trapped bird.

Then the blackness hulked nearer.

I raised my two-by-four torch but it cast no additional light. The end was nothing but glowing embers now. The beginnings of Frozen Body Syndrome crept up my legs, stole along my arms – but this time more than paralyzing fear kept me rooted to the spot. Logic played its role too. If I got too far from the hay fire, I was a goner. I reached out and poked at the small blaze with my dead torch. A new section of the hay flared to life. Firelight jagged across the snow. The bear stopped moving toward us.

The bale fire grew higher and I saw his massive hump sway as he backed up a step. He woofed, a sharp frustrated bark, and both Kestrel and I jumped. Then finally he turned and faded back into oblivion.

I couldn't breathe – but Kestrel could. I could hear her gasping beside me, reacting a totally different way from the fear we shared. I held the torch high, forgetting it was out, but there was nothing more to illuminate anyway. The hay fire already showed us the snow and the side of the barn and the huge grizzly tracks.

"We need more wood to keep the fires going," I said, my voice sounding all creaky, like I hadn't spoken in years.

"There's a little bit more scrap wood," said Kestrel.

We headed inside the barn to discover that the cows had settled down a bit. The sudden darkness might have startled them, but they were adjusting to it and it probably helped to have the walls stop growling at them too.

Before carrying the last of the scrap lumber outside, I opened Rusty's stall and gave him a pat. He stepped out eagerly, glad to be free. Kestrel tucked the loaf of bread beneath her arm before we headed back out to the fires. We divided the scrap lumber between the two side fires, then sat on flat hay chairs in front of the middle fire and crammed big chunks of bread into our mouths.

As we ate, I couldn't help but scan the darkness for movement. The bear was watching us, I felt certain. I could feel his beady little eyes on us, sending shivers down my back like zaps of lightning. Plus James' growling didn't help. He seemed to prefer glaring into the night and growling to eating the pieces of bread we gave him. Not a comforting sign. But despite James' warnings, both Kestrel and I felt safer than we had for hours. As long as the bear remained afraid of fire, we'd be okay. The cows would be protected.

"We need more firewood," Kestrel said. "Look." She pointed to the left fire. It wasn't burning nearly as briskly anymore. Uh oh.

Automatically, we both looked in the direction of the woodshed, though we couldn't have seen it even if it were midday. The woodshed and the cords of wood stacked inside it were behind the house. How were we going to carry the split wood to our fires without getting eaten?

"Does your dad have any more scrap lumber lying around?" I asked hopefully.

Kestrel shook her head.

"What about other stuff, like fences that might be easy to rip down? Or wood from the lean-to shelter?"

I could see her thinking. "We can use the corral fences," she finally said. The closest rails caught the light, so we'd be safe knocking them off their posts and dragging them to the fires. "Dad won't mind getting new poles from the forest if it saves the cows."

"Sounds good to me," I said hurriedly and stuffed my last chunk of bread into my mouth. It tasted totally delectable, and I could feel my body sucking up the energy and nutrients it was providing. Just in time to work at pulling poles off of fence posts. Inward groan. This was going to be hard work. The poles were nailed to the fence posts and we'd have to free each end of each pole from their respective posts. At least they'd make great firewood. The corrals had been there for years, so the wood would be super dry.

We kicked and pushed at one end of the first pole until the single spike that held it was forced out of the fence post, then we leveraged the pole away from the second post until the second spike released. After dragging the pole to the fire, I tried to place it carefully – but it was heavy and when the wood landed, hay ash and smoke poofed up in a choking cloud. The blaze died a bit more.

"Hurry," Kestrel breathed, and we rushed back for a second pole. Then a third, and finally a fourth. We piled these additions strategically on top of the blackened hay and looked down. A tiny finger of light was playing with the first pole. As we watched, it sent tentacles up along the other poles, testing, probing, and finding fresh tinder. Another pole lit. Kestrel and I breathed a sigh of relief at exactly the same moment, then smiled at each other. This was going to work, and the best thing was, there was a lot of wood in each pole. When the part over the fire burned up, we would have the two ends to throw on the blaze.

"Let's get more on the other fires before they go out too," said Kestrel, propelling us into action.

Removing the poles from the fence posts was grueling work. Some of the spikes didn't want to come out of the posts and did only after squealing with protest, as we jerked and kicked and pulled and pushed and groaned and complained. Despite the fresh energy given to me by the world's most amazing bread, I was ready to drop by the time we had all three fires burning brightly and an additional three poles ready to use.

"I'll be back in a minute. I just want to check on the cows," Kestrel said, sounding as tired as I felt.

"Okay," I replied, flopping down beside the middle fire again.

Kestrel went to the door, told James to stay with me, and slipped inside.

"Come, James," I called, and the collie trotted toward me.

"Ow!" Kestrel's complaint shot through the doorway. I could totally guess what had happened, and a moment later, was proven right. Twilight had firmly, and probably none too gently, pushed Kestrel aside. She continued to shoulder her way through the opening and then trotted toward me across the snow, shaking her head. Kestrel looked out through the door, glared at Twilight's retreating bum, then gave me a small wave and closed the door.

Cows stink, said Twilight. I smiled.

James growled. His hackles raised and he glared at me – or was it past me? I spun around. Snow crunched. Something was walking just outside our circle of light.

James barked a high pitched yip.

The snow creaked again, closer this time. It could only be the grizzly. But we had fires. He was afraid of fire.

I stepped back toward the barn until I bumped into Twilight's shoulder. Her ears were tight back. She lowered her head and snorted, then a dark hoof flashed out and struck the snow. Uh oh, she was getting mad. And she didn't have a halter on. There was no way I could stop her from rushing off into the night and harassing the grizzly.

Do not go after him, I begged. *Can kill you with one swat.*

Twilight snorted again, and inside myself I could feel that she hated that I was right. She wanted sooo much to get that bear. She longed to take chunks out of his backside as he ran for his life. I almost smiled at the image her desire created in my mind, but then the bear growled and all thoughts of smiling vanished.

James erupted into panicked barking, then rushed back and forth in front of Twilight and me, a furry whirlwind.

The fire popped and faded just a bit. The bear stepped forward again, and I could see the shape of his massive shoulders and humped, hairy back.

James yipped even louder and beside me I heard a clacking noise. I didn't have to look to know that Twilight was snapping her teeth together. Again, she struck out with a front hoof.

I yelled and waved my arms. My buddies were doing their best to keep the bear away. I had to do the same.

106

The grizzly stepped toward us again and now dancing, devilish flames reflected in his eyes – as he focused on my filly. And I finally understood why he didn't seem afraid. The sight of Twilight was making him angry all over again; she'd enraged him so much that he'd come near the fire to get her.

Just what we needed, a hungry, massive, furious, *and* obsessed grizzly.

Nearer he stalked. Nearer.

Would we all have time to get inside the barn before he attacked?

Not when he was this close.

Chapter 9

I heard the door creak behind us. "What's wrong with...?" Then Kestrel gasped. She'd seen the bear. "Come inside, Evy!"

The bear stopped.

"Now, Evy!"

The bear raised his head and looked for Kestrel, but couldn't seem to find her.

"Get out of here, bear!" I yelled and waved again. Twilight half reared beside me, then came down hard, struck again, and snorted. James' yip grew higher. "Go back to sleep, bear!"

The bear didn't move.

"Yell at him, Kestrel!"

She yelled. The bear started shifting his weight back and forth on his front paws, his nose in the air. An unseen person entering the mix seemed to have shaken him.

I pulled a pole from the nearest blaze and waved the burning end in the air. Then Kestrel was beside me, grabbing her own burning pole.

The bear woofed and half turned away from us, and then stopped to stare hungrily at the barn behind us. I almost felt sorry for him. Almost.

Instead, I yelled louder, and the bear turned away from us and wandered back into the night.

Suddenly my knees buckled. Kestrel was bending over me in a second.

"Are you okay, Evy?"

I nodded.

"I can't believe he almost came to the fire."

"I'm so glad you came back out," I said, my voice shaking.

"How could I not? James sounded like he was having a heart attack, and then you started yelling like that time Twilight pushed you in the lake."

I couldn't help but laugh.

"I wonder why he was afraid of me though. It seems weird," Kestrel said, as she offered me a hand up.

"I don't know. Maybe your dad is from the Bear Clan or something," I suggested as I rose to my feet. "Maybe you can talk to bears like I can talk to horses, and you didn't even know it."

"If that was true, he would've left last night," she said, grimacing. "I didn't want him here then either. And Dad's First Nations clan is the Wolf Clan."

"Then maybe the bear's scared of yelling wolf people."

"Or of two people waving burning torches in his face."

"Yeah, maybe," I admitted, and turned to give Twilight a hug. "Thanks for not backing down, big girl. Even when it's scary. And you too, buddy," I added, rubbing the thick hair of James' ruff.

"They were amazing. Especially Twilight," said Kestrel. "It's not like horses to stand up to a grizzly."

"I think mustangs do that kind of stuff, if they have to, to protect the weaker members of their herd."

"At least you know where you stand," said Kestrel, a teasing lilt to her voice.

"Thanks," I said and laughed again. But it was true. I knew Twilight saw me and Mom as being the weakest members of her herd, which also included Cocoa,

Rusty, and Loonie, our very old and decrepit German Shepherd.

"So, let's build up the fires again," said Kestrel, moving to get more poles.

And so the night went, with short rests between salvaging poles from the closest corrals. We didn't see hide nor hair of the bear during any of our ventures to collect wood, but we knew he was still out there, watching for his opportunity. Twilight and James kept us informed with their super senses.

Neither Kestrel nor I had a watch and so how long we had until dawn remained a mystery. At one point though, I wondered if day would ever come. It seemed we were trapped in a dark dream that would last forever and with a predator that would never sleep. I had a couple of catnaps beside the fire, and I think Kestrel did too, and that helped, but as the night wore on, we became more and more exhausted. Our movements became mechanical and Kestrel and I became quieter. No more encouraging words. No more trying to keep each other's spirits up. Just slogging through snow, straining and kicking and fighting to free a pole from the fence posts, dragging the pole to the smallest fire and throwing it on, tossing in unburned ends, resting for a few minutes – and then starting again. Over and over and over. Eternal. Everlasting. Endless.

Dragging myself through the snow toward the ravaged fence for the billionth time, head down and feeling more beaten than ever before in my life, times about a million, my body aching and sore and longing to fall into the snow to curl up and sleep, sleep, sleep, I suddenly bounced off a gold and black bum.

Twilight, my guard, had stopped right in front of me. She was looking off toward the distant mountains – and suddenly I realized I could *see* Twilight. And not only that, I could see the mountains.

"It's over!" I yelled, probably sounding a little deranged.

Kestrel shrieked and spun around. The pole end that she'd just picked up went flying through the air and almost hit poor James.

"I said, it's over," I said.

She looked at me, not understanding. "What do you mean, it's over?"

"I mean, it's getting light. And I don't see the bear anywhere."

All emotion drained from Kestrel's face. "You mean, he left? We won?"

I turned a complete circle. The dawn's light was brightening the yard. Slowly, the house, remaining corrals, and distant cow pasture drew from the shadows. But no bear.

James left Kestrel's side and ranged out into the yard, sniffing the snow as he went. He trotted on toward the cow pasture, then through the big open space in the fence that the cows had made just yesterday. It seemed like years ago.

Bear gone? I asked Twilight.

Twilight turned to touch me with her muzzle, and then before I could hug her or pet her or show her how much I appreciated her in every imaginable way, she trotted off. She loped around the entire perimeter of the ranch yard, then followed James toward the cow pasture, through the hole, and on into the trees.

"Twilight's checking to make sure he's gone," I told Kestrel.

My friend barely raised her head to look at me. In fact, everything about her seemed to droop. "You look beat," she said.

I almost giggled; I guess I was doing some drooping too. "Do you think it might be safe to sleep?" I asked.

"I don't know."

"Well, let's get Rusty and Twitchy out of the barn anyway. They can eat their breakfast out in the fresh air."

"Okay, but just in case, I'm going to phone for help first," said Kestrel.

"Good idea, but I think it's over. It *feels* over."

"I think so too."

Gone, said Twilight. *Into woods*. She paused. *Before dawn*.

I smiled and told Kestrel the news. She didn't say anything in response but she didn't need to. I understood exactly how she felt because I felt the same. Our relief was too big for words. It really was over. We *had* won, and did victory ever feel sweet!

Finally, Kestrel moved toward the house. "I'll go phone now," she said, her voice lighter.

"I'll get some hay down for the horses," I said, though all I wanted to do was sit by the fire and bask in our victory.

Walking back into the barn almost bowled me over. *Stinky* was an understatement. One hundred and twenty-one warm, poopy cows, kept in an enclosed space can create quite the smell. But then I saw Freda, with her pristine white face and deer-like eyes, being guarded by her mom. She was sooo cute I didn't notice the smell as much after that.

Rusty greeted me, putting his velvet nose on my cheek and blowing. I stood still and closed my eyes, then reached to give him a hug. He'd been such a big help too. We couldn't have done any of this without him, Twilight, and James. And Twitchy too, though she hadn't done much last night but sleep.

She was awake now for sure though. She whinnied impatiently from her stall, and I moved past Rusty to free her, stopping first to check on Bella. The cow glared across her stall at me, probably still mad because I'd sat on her last night. Of course, Twitchy glared at me too. Apparently, I wasn't fetching her breakfast quite quickly enough.

The barn door opened behind us and I turned to see Kestrel enter the barn.

"That didn't take long," I said.

"Mom and Dad have already left the hotel to come home, so I phoned Charlie. He'll be here in a couple of hours."

"That's good. He'll know what to do about the bear."

"I think it'll probably have to be put down," Kestrel said, her voice sad.

"Probably." The idea made me sad too. Though the bear was vicious and dangerous, he was still a living creature. Unfortunately, he wasn't willing to let the rest of us live in peace. If he was, he'd be perfectly safe right now.

Kestrel moved to Twitchy's stall and slipped the halter on the mare's head, then led her from the barn. A couple of cows tried to squeeze through the doors behind her, but Rusty sent them back with a snaking head and yellow teeth before exiting himself. Cows aren't overly bright, as I've said, but they'd learned a new appreciation of horse bites since yesterday.

I yawned and moved to the loft ladder, then climbed up and swished through the loose hay to the outside loft doors and threw them wide. Two hungry horses looked up at me from below. In the distance, I felt Twilight become aware that breakfast was being served at Kestrel's house, and seconds later, she galloped from the forest.

I threw the bales out and Kestrel cut the twine and removed the strings. Then she looked up at me and smiled. "After we give the cows their breakfast, we should sleep in the loft."

"That sounds perfect. The horses will wake me if the bear comes back, and we'll be right here if he does."

Twilight ran around Kestrel, acting afraid that she might try to halter her. Weird horse. Why would Kestrel want to keep her from her breakfast?

My friend just laughed, and a minute later, she was inside the barn again, climbing the ladder. Together we threw more hay into the arena and spread it around for the cows, then checked their water. There was still a bit in the big trough, enough so we could get some sleep before having to refuel the generator and pump water into the massive container.

At last, we pushed the loose hay in the loft into two big piles to make soft beds and collapsed. I hardly had the energy to pull more hay over my aching body. Then I shut my eyes and slept.

"Evy!"

Huh? What did Kestrel want?

"Kestrel!"

Just let me sleep.

"EVY! KESTREL!"

Mom? I rose out of my hay bed. "Mom?"

Of course she couldn't hear me. I was in the loft and she didn't sound too close to the barn. She was just being loud. I hurried toward the loft doors and again threw them wide. Mom was mounted on Cocoa with Loonie and Rusty at her side. Loonie and James were sniffing each other's butts, becoming reacquainted.

"Mom!" I yelled, and she turned on Cocoa's back to look for me.

I waved to help her find us, then shouted, "We'll be right down."

It took a minute to wake Kestrel, but once I did and she realized Mom was there, she beat me to the ladder. The cows were all resting as we rushed through the barn. We were going to have to get their pasture fence fixed soon so we could turn them out again, but first things first.

Mom was at the barn, dismounting Cocoa, when we burst outside. Moments later, we were in her arms.

"What happened? Why did Rusty come get me?"

My heart glowed. Rusty must have opened the ranch gate somehow and gone all the way home to let Mom know we needed help. Or Twilight opened it for him. That made more sense. She probably wanted out so she could go adventure seeking again, no doubt thinking that yesterday's adventure was so over.

You are awesome! I raved to Rusty.

Yes.

I laughed. It was his usual response.

"What's so funny?" asked Mom.

Oops, that laugh was out loud. "Sorry, Mom. It's just the stress."

"What happened to the corrals? Why are the cows in the barn? And these fires." She pulled away from Kestrel and me and searched my eyes, then must have realized that this explanation was going to take a while. "Let's go inside and you can tell me all about it."

"But the cows..." said Kestrel.

"The cows will be fine in the barn for another hour. Come inside."

It seemed so weird to leave them alone. After all we'd gone through together, I felt like I was abandoning them. What if the bear chose that moment to come roaring back into the yard? What if something else bad happened? We were their protectors, whether they liked us or not. Bella's glare flashed into my mind and I giggled again. Mom looked back at me with concern and Kestrel elbowed me.

It took about half an hour to tell Mom everything, and then she made us eat and sent us to bed, just like we were little kids. Of course, I didn't mind until after I woke up. And even then, being treated like a kid didn't matter so much when I found the house empty and walked out onto the porch to see the pasture fence fixed and the cattle placidly eating their evening meal inside their enclosure. Little Freda bounced around her mom on the edge of the herd, being completely adorable – and beside her, trying to copy her, another new calf. Cool!

Mom and Kestrel were inside the barn, shoveling the last of the cow poo.

"Why didn't you wake me up when you got up?" I asked Kestrel.

Kestrel shrugged. "You looked like you were having good dreams."

"The dream of not shoveling cow dung," said Mom.

"Hey, I would've helped if I wasn't sleeping."

"I'm just teasing you, kiddo. Really, you deserve a lot more than getting out of cleaning the barn," said Mom. "What you two did, keeping the cattle safe, that was amazing."

"Really?"

"Yes, really."

"I guess it *was* kind of hard," Kestrel said, trying unsuccessfully to sound modest.

"Kind of." Mom laughed.

"Just a little."

James barked outside, and a moment later, Loonie joined him.

My heart spiked in my throat. The bear! It was back!

Rumbly people, said Twilight from wherever she was hanging out. That's her way of saying people in a vehicle.

"Someone's coming. Maybe it's Charlie," I said, though that didn't seem right. Usually he rode Redwing.

"Charlie showed up hours ago," said Mom. "And he didn't waste any time going after the bear."

"It's Mom and Dad!" Moments later, Kestrel was out the door.

I hurried after her.

"Evy, wait," said Mom.

"Yeah?"

"Come here."

When I reached her, Mom drew me into a big hug and then bent to kiss my forehead. She doesn't have to bend down far these days. I'm almost as big as she is, even though I'm still only thirteen. Almost fourteen.

"Before we go out there, there's something I want to say. What you and Kestrel did, I'm not kidding, it was amazing. I am so blown away and impressed by both of you."

I smiled into Mom's shoulder. "Thanks, Mom."

"I hope you can always be so clear-headed. And so brave."

"Um, I'll try."

"You're so strong. In the future, if things happen, I hope you can always look at things reasonably."

Okay, so this was just getting weird. I pulled back to look into her eyes. "Something's going to happen?"

"No, no. I'm not saying that," she said, suddenly all evasive. "Not at all. I'm just... I... I don't know what I'm saying."

And then I got it. She was talking about the secret of why the two of us were living in the bush. Did this mean she was finally going to tell me who she was hiding from? And why? And why the hiding out probably had something to do with me?

"If there's anything you want to tell me, of course I can be brave about that too," I said, hoping that my earlier cluelessness hadn't thrown her off.

She searched my gaze for one long second and then her eyes shifted to the door. Outside we could hear Kestrel excitedly telling her parents what had happened while they were gone.

"Mom? You can tell me anything, you know," I said, trying to pull her attention back to more important stuff.

But when she looked back at me, it was obvious she wasn't going to say a word. I could see it in her eyes. Yes, she was impressed by what Kestrel and I had done, but it wasn't enough to convince her to tell me our history.

"I know I can, Evy," she said, her words light and without meaning. "Now let's get out there and say hi." She walked past me toward the door.

I didn't move. Instead, I stared at the back of the barn and blinked away tears of frustration. She'd been so close to telling me. Closer than ever before.

"Come on."

I turned to see her waiting for me in the doorway, and her eyes seemed sad, as if she too knew that we'd missed something special, as if she was sorry she couldn't muster the courage to tell me yet.

As I walked toward her, she smiled apologetically and my mood lightened. I'm an optimist, after all. I still may not know why she'd brought us to this wild place to live, I may not know who she was hiding from or why, but I knew that she trusted my abilities just a little bit more now. Her respect for me had grown, and as time went on and I grew up, she'd learn to have faith in my ability to cope with the hard things.

When I reached her, she took my arm, and we walked into the yard together. Confidence filled me as we strode toward Kestrel and her parents. For the first time ever, I had no doubt. I *would* know the answers to Mom's mystery someday. Maybe someday soon. Either she would tell me or I would discover the answer and she would confirm it. Maybe even this spring, when she had to go on her agent search – as long as I could find a way to make her take me with her.

This mystery was like an apple ripening on a tree. Someday it would fall.

Apple? asked Twilight, and I could feel her mouth tingle with anticipation. *Where apple?*

I laughed. Actually, an apple or two would taste pretty good right now.

What will happen next?

Please turn the page

for a sneak preview

of the next book

Whinnies on the Wind
Volume 6

<u>Spring of Secrets</u>

Available at:

www.ponybooks.com

When Evy's mom decides to take a trip to the city, Evy is thrilled. Finally, she'll get to investigate some of her mom's mysteries. But then her mom says she must stay behind.

Yeah, right!

With the help of some mustangs, Evy stows away in the back of her mom's borrowed truck and heads out on the wildest ride of her life, where she'll meet a foal in trouble and a horse who looks like an angel. She'll find adventure, a new friend, and answers – answers so mystifying they might as well be questions.

CPSIA information can be obtained
at www.ICGtesting.com
Printed in the USA
BVHW051157180721
612146BV00010B/1033